HIDDEN LANDS BEYOND THE ANTARCTICA

The Continuation of Morris' Journey Between the Interconnected Planets

CLAUDIO NOCELLI

CLAUDIO ÁNGEL NOCELLI

ISBN: 978-987-88-9328-0

Printed in the United States of America

CONTENTS

WEBSITE:

https://nosconfunden.com.ar/

YOUTUBE:

https://www.youtube.com/
@nosconfunden

YOUTUBE SECUNDARIO:

https://www.youtube.com/
@nosconfundieron

INSTAGRAM:

https://www.instagram.com/
nosconfunden/

INSTAGRAM PERSONAL DEL AUTOR:

https://www.instagram.com/
eddienosconfunden/

(In the case of not being able to enter any of the social networks due to any error, they will always be updated in the main website, you can visit it to be informed about possible updates, thank you very much for your understanding)

Nocelli, Claudio Ángel
Hidden Lands Beyond the Antarctica : The Continuation of Morris_ourney Between the Interconnected Planets / Claudio Ángel Nocelli. - 1a ed. - Ciudad Autónoma de Buenos Aires : Claudio Ángel Nocelli, 2023.
97 p. ; 16 x 23 cm.

Traducción de: Claudio Ángel Nocelli.
ISBN 978-987-88-9328-0

1. Ciencia Ficción. 2. Cuentos de Aventuras. 3. Ovnis. I. Título.
CDD A863

CHAPTER 1 - THE FORGOTTEN HEROES

In this day and age, looking at that white mantle of walls as a gateway seems far-fetched, and today, very few dare to do so, one of the paths could be found by digging deep into the true agenda that hides in the dark minds of the dome that in turn plays intertwined with the archaic and parasitic colonizers of yesterday, those who treacherously penetrated the Domes and poured their plans into our kingdom, and so it is and will be, as I say, ours forever.

Antarctica brings with it the mystery of those questions as old as humanity itself, only that sometimes it is clouded among so many news and information that run from beginning to end in the mainstream media that end up accumulating almost by obligation in our minds riddled with news that hide other motives behind that thick fog of those who rule today, I say today, but I could also say the not so distant yesterday, although every day seems like a dagger stabbing into the hearts of true humanity, the agony of living in a cold and unjust world, these writings are not simply stories for you and me to empathize with our reality, they are mere parts of a puzzle that we can put together if we really try, they are parts of our stolen history, our brothers who died fighting for our future, for a different one, and today we forget them simply because we were sold a different story since we were children, the human ancestors and the giants sleep in the hearts of those who really want to remember, of those who still want a fair and different world from today, from this macabre, gloomy, unjust and sometimes repulsive present, these writings will remain forever for those restless minds that are not satisfied with what they were told, with those who debate in front of them according to the books that are kept under golden domes, the fictitious titles that some organizations wanted to grant, nor those who have been meeting to change the world for many years and who do little or nothing or achieve, simply because the reality is that they do not try to do it either.

You and I can change it, and I affirm it without any doubt and in spite of the adversity that you may find on your way, even in some of the stories that you will find right here in these writings, as I always say you should question everything, even you should not believe anything of all this just stay with the parts that resonate within you, just follow your heart and investigate from there without prejudice and absolute freedom about the reality that surrounds you, and then from there gathering those parts left to us of this great puzzle, joining key pieces, understanding what was the Great War between the colonizing parasites and the true ancestral heroes, this is the beginning of a unique journey that you as a reader can join me and follow the same course of the beginning of your great change, today can be that day, there is no need to wait for it, just let it happen, come on! No being on this plane deserves to be trapped in a parasitic conquest, we all deserve to be born and live free until the return to the Celestial Lands.

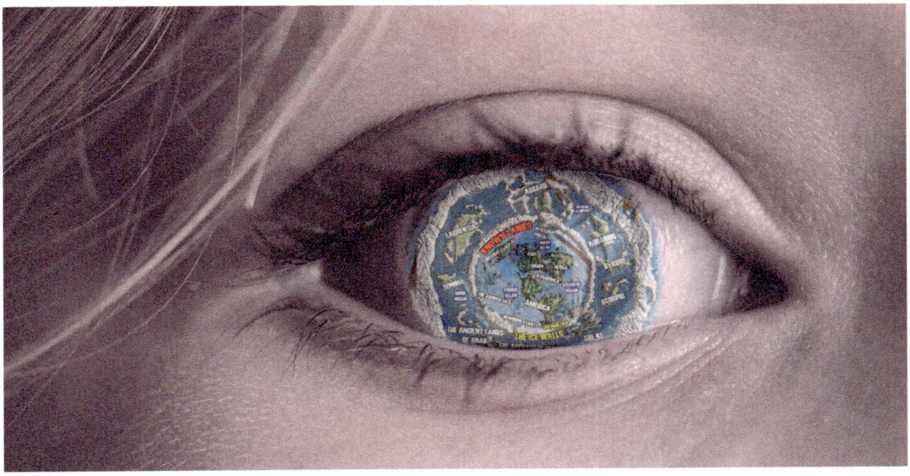

CHAPTER 2 – THE ENCOUNTER WITH HELEN MORRIS

On the shores of a beach far from the big cities, under a harsh winter weather, everything was desolate, the cold was my only company at that moment when suddenly everything became strange, the movements around me had become slower and the colors looked more vivid and I could even distinguish their thousands of shades perfectly.

I closed my eyes and then I felt how a diffuse figure that seemed feminine was approaching, everything happened very slowly, the following sensations cannot be explained with words, it was like seeing a hologram in front of me, even with my eyes closed, the image was there.

- It's not so long ago that I have seen you and you already look older, huh, how are you still seeing this world? She asked in an angelic voice, very hard to mistake. Besides the question and the strange situation surrounding the experience I understood perfectly who it was.

- Helen! Her name came out from inside me, as my heart was suddenly racing.

HM - So, won't you answer my question dear friend?

- "Humanity in here is most complex," I was able to say and then added, "But, when united for a real reason their strengths don't seem to fade easily, at least that's what I learned from a mysterious woman who claimed to come from afar" I smiled staring at this strange "holographic specter" of hers.

HM - "That's totally valid, a phrase that seems to come from someone intelligent," she smiled now complicit in my earlier joke, then continued:

- "It's a pity that many are forced to take equivocal paths then don't you think so?" I nodded, and though I dared not until then express more than that.

- "When did you come?" I asked excitedly. Her eyes penetrated my being like two lighthouses dazzling the sight of a navigator finding new lands, an inexplicable feeling of love invaded my body.

HM - Things are getting difficult again, I sense that many of this new humanity already know it, it is not my function to alarm anyone nor do I intend to, but have you seen everything that has been happening here lately? We follow it closely. "I think you already understand it well, time is the most precious thing and when it comes to such a sensitive issue as freedom, which is paramount, something has to be activated within all of us."

- How could I help? I asked.

HM - You are already doing your part, it is the right time for all the information we possess to be revealed, or at least what is important, about the lands outside the Dome and the first ice walls, reaching the right point we may have a new opportunity to carry out the Morris-Butler plan, the parasitic agenda has not slowed down from a few years ago to here, it is constant and seems to have no other outcome in their plans, they have already decided long ago, the fate of the new humanity depends strictly on the changes that can be made from here to the future, you understand, Don't you?

- Do you think that there are some of those points in this "parasitic agenda" that are inevitable? I asked her fearfully for an answer that seemed to be known in advance.

HM - I prefer to think not, but I would be lying to you, the situation is worrying, and it could not only reach these lands, it could reach ours too, the ones outside this "First Dome".

- I opened my eyes as wide as I could... How is it possible that a new reset could also damage humanity outside?

HM - It is a possibility, not all resets are alike, indirectly it would affect us anyway, we need to unite and stay on the indicated plan, there is no margin for error this time, nothing can fail. But excuse me for interrupting this talk, I will go directly to what I came to tell you, do not forget that being in these lands generates me a deep pain and not only in a physical way since my body hurts being here, but stepping on these lands always make me have mixed thoughts and feelings, on the one hand the joy of seeing my brothers of the new humanity and on the other the idea that we could not achieve yet what we so longed for, human freedom from the parasitic hands that today still control it, I see my father's face every day here repeating that phrase, but, as I said before, let's go to the point of this meeting, there are many topics to know about my father William, let's continue from where we had left that time about his interesting and mysterious journey.

CHAPTER 3 - THE ANCESTORS RETURN TO THE KNOWN LANDS

- William, wake up! It's time to put the plan into action, look to the sky "The Iron Blues" are advancing! Don't abandon us now your brothers need you... Butler's voice rang like bells from an ancient church in my poor confused mind. I know I had received some kind of injection to revive my slowly fading body.

"My brothers" that word made my body detach from the cold sand that hugged me tightly so as not to let go, but even if this was my last breath I had to be on my feet, helped clearly by what

Butler had given me as I lay unconscious on the shore of the beautiful ancestral beaches.

- William, up mate, look around you, it's time now. Butler sentenced with a small phrase that swept everything inside me, it was like those devastating waves that can take everything in its path.

I knew how important it was for me and for many of us such an event, the "Iron Blues" and thousands of ships were going straight to the "Ice Walls", those artificial frozen walls that forbade our brothers to see a new dawn, the radiant red Sun that contemplated an advanced civilization like the Ancestral one, where I already felt part of it, of survivors who fought long ago against the same yoke that today possesses the new humanity in various ways, that keeps them living a simulation full of lies, that offers them only a tiny part of an absolute happiness that they could live understanding that they are "The Source" and the great importance under this great Dome.

That your energy is so rooted in the "Celestial Lands" that so many other Worlds keep close track of it, and jealously imprison you within these cold walls that act as a division, today permanent, next to the "First Dome". If only they knew their true past and the purpose of their creation, that they were born to be free and to fight against this snatching of freedoms towards their own race and towards the others, they were all born to be heroes, each one in his own way, and not to compete in a hostile world among their own brothers for a piece of bread, for thirsty drops of power, for an absolute and spiritual existential void, I have it clear because I have lived there and I have felt the same as each one of you can feel.

My body was less sore, but partially numbed by the ancestral medication that keeps me alive hopefully for some more time, and the time I have left I will absolutely use it around the liberation of my brothers, of a humanity that can step as hard as those giants that crossed the same ice to help us wake up. Long live the awakened humanity that fights for its own spiritual freedom! I shouted inside me, who knows why, but I felt that internal euphoria, although no one heard it, it emboldened me for what was to come.

Thousands of Ancestors were already crossing the borders towards the "Known Lands", those continents that since we were children we were taught and somehow forced to understand that it was the only thing we had, since according to the official books, the famous Christopher Columbus had discovered that "New Continent" that would mark a before and an after, It would pale in comparison to what I discovered on my journey with my old ship, which crossed the famous "Antarctic Polar Circle" and took me to lands I never thought I knew, that I could never even have dreamed of. How could a remote place give me so many answers and so much peace along the way?

Only that my peace was intermingled with that intrinsic pain that means leaving my lands of origin and the knowledge of what was happening behind, but this would be nothing if I knew that my brothers were in good hands or in total freedom, but that all suffering in there came from the dirty parasitic hands that had stolen the eternal spiritual growth of our own race, humanity was imprisoned between walls, false stories, maps and a very uncertain path to follow, the many resets suffered and the thousands of generations waiting for a peace that would hardly come being under the same Custodian power, which for thousands and thousands of years (in Known Lands) submerged us in an absolute confusion about our creation, true mission and resentment towards the "other brother".

This story has just begun, but it is a unique path that you will walk together with me, you can believe it or not, it all depends on your inner self, but here I will try to give you some details about the worlds surrounding our Known Lands, the way I learned about them from the teaching of the ancestral masters themselves as well as from the thousands of stories and records that exist in the Ancestral Library here in these lands, but let's go in parts, we still have a long way to go.

CHAPTER 4 - THE ICE WALLS AND THE FIRST DOME

My great friend and companion in this odyssey, Butler, who was the pioneer and who brought me to these distant lands, had somehow saved my life, had made me know not only the true human purpose, but also had given me a new life, away from the sinister clutches of the old continents, as well as meeting the woman of my life who has given me the most precious gift from the heavens, my daughter Helen.

Starting from scratch in other lands, trying to understand how their technology worked, their society, their way of life, was totally strange and it was a process that lasted a long time for me, but I must admit that it is much easier to adapt to the life of the Ancestors than if I had to go in the opposite direction.

I could not understand how an Ancestor, for more experiences he has had, could undergo the punishment of returning to the "Known Lands", I hope these texts will reach those readers who are more curious about the lands they inhabit, and if these are my brothers from the old continents, I hope they will understand that my absolute wish is that one day the majority of people will understand that they are under this Custodian power that in each past "reset" has poisoned more and more not only our bodies but also our minds, the way of life has been getting worse as these resets have been carried out.

When I speak of "resets" I am referring to the sudden and abrupt endings, always in a cruel way, that are generated in the known continents to the different times that humanity lives and has lived through the times since its beginning, these resets that we contemplate throughout human history would be seven (counting the clash of the first humans in Asgard-Hyperborea against the Custodians).

Here they call them different generations, the ancestral ones lived in the "Known Lands" or "Old Continents" after the "Sixth Reset" that took place the Great War between Giant-Humans, Humans, and other races against the Custodians, Anunnaki and part of the race of the "Greys" that many came from Orion and others were settled here while carrying out what would be one of the largest and best equipped civilizations of all times of mankind in those lands that we have record of, The Great Tartary.

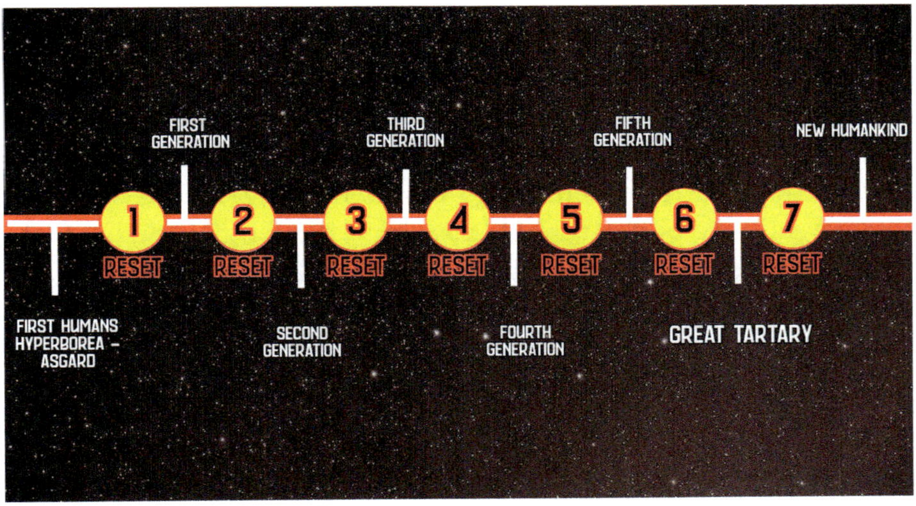

The great veil that does not allow approaching the "First Dome" and that extends throughout the geographical region covering the "Circle-Environment" of the "Earth" as you know it, was planned and carried out during the sixth generation, more specifically, during the advance of the Great Tartary, that with its technology that came from "outside" better said, the use of "extraterrestrial technology" that transferred both in knowledge and prototypes a part of the race of Giants, called "Anakim", and also another race of Giant-Humans of the fifth generation (this I will explain later).

There is nothing worse that derives to hell itself as "Resets", and they can happen in several ways, the Anunnaki helped to install their Pyramids for the development and capacity to be able to generate great floods throughout the Known Lands in a fast and better controlled way, each pyramid can act both as a projector to the "Sky-Dome" and act in a "holographic image" creating way as well as scanning large portions of land for different types of statistics, both of the soil and the environment itself, regulating the climate and toxins that may or may not affect a certain group of humans, as well as having a great impact on the human mind.

This was advancing since the third generation of humans, when the Anunnaki put their parasitic hands and helped the Custodian control and manipulation in all these lands, and as they improved their technology it was no longer necessary for the pyramids to be scattered throughout the length and breadth of the continents, Although in use they had a direct impact and were used, they were used more for urgency than for a technological issue, since they control the weather and almost everything inside the Ice Walls themselves very well.

The Walls were created by them not only in these lands, but in many other worlds that we can find crossing the different Domes and other barriers that can appear in our way.

The incorporation of the use of "Portals" was key in their race to conquer other worlds as well as the manipulation of these, to be able to advance in their desire to know the mysterious lands behind the "Great Dome" that, apparently, are connected in an intrinsic way to the "Celestial Lands" or "Terra-Incognita".

THE ANCESTRAL BOOKS OF THE SACRED LIBRARY

CHAPTER 5 - THE BOOKS ABOUT THE HIDDEN LANDS

Before beginning this extensive tour, I must clarify several points that are necessary, and that may also be enlightening when we go through it later. All the information that we have gathered and that you can find in one of our most precious buildings in the city of "El Arca" or "The Ark" and "Renacer", where Morris visited thousands of times during his extensive stay in the Ancestral Lands, is simply a tiny part of a great puzzle, which although it is true that it is more complete and can be visited by any ancestral citizen, unlike those of the new humanity (which most of them do not know), we must also take into account that we still have a lot to know, even from the same Custodian or Anunnaki dome that are trying to unveil some mysteries today about everything that surrounds the Celestial Lands and what is behind the Great Dome.

They answered anyway the deepest questions that seemed to haunt about the great mystery of the existence of the beings "down here", but, now is not the time to give you more information so as not to overwhelm you, this information you do not need for now.

I think the best to start this path as once the same Giant-Human called "She-Ki" taught my dear father William, the stories of the ancients will explain several important points of the lands that are unknown to you today, we have an extensive part of our Library with all the stories of those heroes, both ancestral and human of previous generations, including other stories that were taken in the great Custodian centers where many Giants and Giant-Humans entered during the Great War, custodian reports that explain many phenomena, such as the use of portals, hidden lands and the famous "planets" as you know them.

What I meant before with "the vast majority is unaware" is that there are groups of people who are aware of various custodian phenomena and plans that are carried out daily, even on other lands and I would dare say on custodian technology as well, in fact it has been and is delivered to this day to members who are in the highest spheres, secret organizations and several people of the forces that have possibly traveled and been in other "planets" or even lands that surround their walls, some have returned and others have not, among all the stories that you will read below you will find several of these characters that for favors done against their own brothers, have won a passage to other places, some of them as recondite as that of their dark minds that worked to harm their own race.

These texts have never been violated nor have they been exposed to other people who have not been our Anakim brothers or ancestral humans, therefore do not alter them, they have never left our lands and today it is time to do so, with a great purpose and destiny, which is neither mine nor their own, but that of the millions of humans who are born in "Walled Lands" without being able to even stop to think about the ground they walk on, because they have not left you, because they outrage you, they punish you, they inhibit you, they restrain you, they empty you spiritually from the primary schools to later make you compete among yourselves to see which one gets the prize of eating too much, eating and not eating at all, they play with your stomachs, with your minds, with your hope, as they played with your great grandparents, grandparents, parents, siblings, etc.

These texts are an intrinsic part to find the forgotten path of our past and our greatness, it will be up to you to draw your own conclusions about the stories that are expressed here, as well as to differentiate the many lies that some will bring to light later in reference to these books both about the lands that were kept hidden for the new humanity, as well as many other topics related to the ancient civilizations, the resetting, and the colonizing parasites, as they will most likely try to manipulate and erase these stories throughout these years that will be sent by the same Custodians who will try to prevent this knowledge and the final liberation.

We will never determine what you should or should not believe, you should always investigate on your own and follow what your heart feels without any conditioning, but be aware, about everything that is opposite to the most important, about the infinite spiritual potential of the human being and his freedom.

Knowing this reality at least you will be closer to be able to see all that we are exposing here, freedom is only one and can be obtained in many ways, such as fighting, but the fight is not physical as we learned in the "Great War" where human freedom was sought and obtained only a reset of new human slaves of their own lands, then the path has to be spiritual, if the mental chains are broken then you will be in a place that not many were, at least in this humanity, where the cold parasites rule, you can even travel to that place without lifting a finger.

CHAPTER 6 - RESETS, THE LAST STEP TOWARDS TOTAL DESTRUCTION

"Resets" or "Restarts" are undoubtedly one of the major concerns of both us and most other civilizations and worlds around us who are aware of the current human situation. For those who are not aware, a "Reset/Restart" as its word indicates is to carry out an abrupt ending to make room for a new beginning, but if you still believe that "a new beginning" is something productive or healthy, I regret to inform you that in this case your illusions will be shattered into thousands of pieces, because this is almost always carried out in the worst possible way, hostile, bloody, cold, violent and all the terrifying qualifications that we could use here to catalog such an aberration before life, and before, in this case, humanity.

This interruption to human progress is always carried out in the worst way and the motives are not positive either, after each "Reboot" there would always be enormous changes with modification in the human mind and body, as well as modification of the environment.

The Anunnaki-Custodian technology was advancing so much that it was more and more difficult to miss anything. These "Resets" are carried out by the same parasitic races since the beginning of their colonization here in these lands, but as we were saying, they were intensifying each time they were carried out, one after another, because either humanity itself took the pressure to the maximum level to know its true essence, the worlds and civilizations that surround it in conjunction with the dirty parasitic hands it has on it, or it was carried out by the latter, or it was carried out by the latter in their eagerness to abruptly end a war, a large scale revolt, or simply an advance in technology worrying to the power, "the power of the known power" we could call it, since it does not matter too much the faces or bodies we know that may be at the front in those unreachable domes, they are always or almost always dominated by the same Custodian-Anunnaki power.

Of the Seven Known Resettings, the most serious and the one that was carried out the worst based on the bloody and hostile, added to the change that humanity would have next, was the last one, and it was carried out to annihilate the great heroes of the "Great Tartary" as well as the humans who followed fervently and had understood what the true desire to be free and all that this meant.

Once the Southern Giants or "Anakim" penetrated from behind the so-called "South Pole" or rather "South Portal" they immediately began their plan to liberate humanity by providing technology that the sixth generation human had never seen, as well as information from outside the First Dome.

The Custodians who had had an epic battle against the Anunnaki during that period where the Giants took the opportunity to intermingle on the old continents, had to once again come to a treaty agreement with the Anunnaki to help them with this great problem that had arisen during their absence on their most treasured colony.

They had left an inferior race of Orion Greys, who, although they surpassed humans in technology, the colony had simply not been guarded as it should have been, it is still unknown if it was intentional or not, but since then the relationship they had with the Custodians for trusting them and not fulfilling the assigned tasks guarding their great colony was to change forever and take a course of no return.

The Giant-Humans, Anakim Giants and Humans of the sixth generation began to die in different ways, both in the same battles in the many air attacks to the great cities-cores as well as different "climatic disasters" would begin to happen and help the annihilation of every being that stepped on the known lands. The deaths were counted very well to reach the needed number of "Reboot", the babies were prepared in their great hidden laboratories to proceed to inhabit the "new human dawn" in the seventh generation.

The new humanity would begin, I mean, our humanity was beginning to emerge. During great battles, heroes both giant and ancestral perishing in what would be epic memories of yesterday trying to change the course of a sleeping humanity, the Great Tartary would fall along with its great technology based on free energy, and its many dreams shattering into pieces against the cold ocean watered with blood.

Many of the humans were able to slip away and escape along with the Anakim through the passages or portals that led to the other lands behind the First Dome, despite the great floods and eternal roads to them, some of them survived and even today continue to tell their stories, the parents of my dear wife, and she herself who even as a baby of just months could escape in the arms of her mother to an uncertain future but that gave her some hope to start again in other lands away from their origin, but also away from the terror that was being lived. Undoubtedly then, this last recorded restart was the crudest of all for the way it was given and for the sorrow of feeling that we were very close to winning that great battle for freedom and that everything came to nothing with devastating consequences for the new humanity to come, our own, my brothers, who continue to struggle daily to free themselves knowing it or not, from that world that they were told that it must be like that, that they were manipulated that it cannot be changed, that they were given in a rain of lies with absolute bad intentions to leave them on their knees since childhood, they can still get up, I still know in my heart that humanity lives and dreams more than ever with a possible freedom, and we from here, believe me, that we will try everything until the end of our days.

CHAPTER 7 - THE PETRIFIED TREES, THE SOUTHERN GIANTS AND THE CONNECTION WITH FIFTH GENERATION HUMANITY

Why did the Anakim Giants and other race of Giants decide to assist in the liberation of mankind?

It is a great question that haunted my mind over and over again, throughout my studies here in these lands with the ancestral brothers who gave me from the beginning a warm welcome (although as you know it was quite traumatic as soon as we arrived) where I was, somehow, sharing with the same ancestor of our new humanity and where I also took advantage of my closeness to, at least, be able to clear some of my concerns.

While it could be understood that the Anakim simply saw

the opportunity to infiltrate at a propitious moment during that confrontation between the conquerors themselves, the Custodian-Anunnaki War, it is also true that much was risked in that movement of jumping across into hell itself by beings who perhaps were not even aware of their true essence.

I felt that something had to motivate them beyond what was explained superficially and the understanding that each one could have acquired from this fact, She-Ki knew how to give me the answer some time later, after my permanent insistence to be able to contact her again, I needed to ask her several questions and one night finally came what I longed for so much.

She-Ki confessed to me that the Anakim or Giants of the South, have human blood running through their veins from a remote past. During the "Fifth Generation", that is, prior to the Ancestors, and that, in turn, that same blood some also share with another more primitive Giant race, there being a direct connection with the lands of Asgard, all this was again like a bomb exploding in my mind with fresh information that could dispel great clouds of uncertainty, each word of She-Ki became more and more interesting and began somehow to close many paths in my confused mind.

The human physical build was very different, so was the way time was passing as well as the environment in the "Known Lands".

A handful of Anakim Giants and a few of another Giant race decided in those times past to overcome the First Dome to infiltrate the human lands, a little out of curiosity and a little to see the possibility they had to infiltrate some information as well as technology. They did it through what we know as "South" side of our lands, and settled there for a long time, in many manipulated books they can be found even today as "Patagonian Giants", although the dates are incorrect as well as the image of them that would be publicly known.

These beings began to feel part of these lands and to get closer to the humans that also lived there, and since then they simply began to develop. Although their bodies began to get sick, this did not happen until many years after their first visit, as they were not fully aware of the toxins that could rain down from the heavens themselves.

They came to make large fortifications in the closest part of the known "Antarctic Peninsula" between what is known today as Argentina and Chile, in addition to other lands that do not appear on current maps and all the way to the islands that were there at that time.

The Giants began to explore "the old continents" and the hidden lands (many of them disappeared between the floods by later resets) and surprisingly discovered trees of colossal sizes, they began to understand that the human past was totally different to what they understood until then, these colossal trees were difficult to locate in human history, they did not fit directly, the first humans coming from Asgard, Lemuria and Atlantis had to have not only used them but "planted" themselves with some purpose, now, what kind of energy or connection did they have? Were they used in some way as Portals or to hide another type of technology? Who or who had given those "seeds" or knowledge to obtain these mysterious trees to the ancient humans?

Many questions hovered around this issue and the Giants surely came to a conclusion, for that reason they decided to settle there and even enlarge their population without attracting so much attention from the ruling Custodians, perhaps their answer was rooted in the beginning of humanity and its connection with the Celestial Lands.

The trees during that reset were cut down, destroyed (burned, pulverized) or petrified with Custodian technology, many of them we find today along the known continents, many others are taken as simple hills, mountains or even mountain ranges, then we will understand better what happened to these Giants as well as to the humanity of the Fifth Generation later on.

There are still some memories left in the ancient books of the old continents about, for example, "Medusa", that monster that turned into stone those who dared to look directly into her eyes, it was a faithful reflection of a clear message "the one who drew the veil of the dark dome would be stone for all eternity".

Besides being metaphorical, the idea that beings could be petrified is somehow established in the Known Lands but certainly always in the form of mythology or stories far from reality, it is quite complex to understand that giant beings or titans have also been petrified throughout human generations, perhaps many of them sought to free "The Source" for the kingdoms to restore their peace, let's not forget that the colonizing parasites soon invaded many of the worlds even when the beings of each environment were developing, therefore, it was easily accessible for them to conquer almost all of them, with exceptions of course, but sooner or later they would obtain the power they have today.

Are there mountains or mountains that are ancient petrified beings? That is a question that I will not answer at this time, but, I have asked She-Ki although it seems crazy to many, I did not want to stay with that intrigue, the truth is that I can confirm that giant trees if they were cut from their bases, some were so huge that today are also considered mountains or forgotten mountains that stand out among the plains or even more spectacular mountains, the bones of enormous beings could have suffered the same fate during their stay in the old continents, simply for trying to change the course of the human generations to come, many of these colossal trees were used as a form of transfer of matter, or better said, natural portals to distant or hidden lands.

CHAPTER 8 - THE GREAT DOME AND THE CELL WALL IN THE 178 WORLDS

As I commented earlier, the Great Dome is the one that "covers" above all the "known worlds", I mean, known and not so known to many of us outside the First Ice Walls, this is key to understand how these worlds could work, I also understand that it may overwhelm you in a direct way at first as you are not even familiar with the lands surrounding your continents, it would be more difficult for you to understand how all of what you know as "planets" can meet in a horizontal direction instead of vertical as drawn by the most prestigious scientists of your Circle-Environment, it is difficult to deal with this idea and believe me, I spent years studying how the First Dome could work and what is projected on it.

Directly speaking "what the heavens show every day". To be able to really interpret how one could "navigate the skies" going directly horizontally to the Poles, or, better said, to the "Antarctic Polar Circle" which is that only physical barrier it has before the direct collision with this barrier-dome, a priori, invisible.

The Dome barrier functions simply as described, a division between one environment and the other, but as something known to you (so far) in your time as is the "cell" in specific parts of its walls there can be a direct connection that mixes or lets pass in a certain way, something from environment A to environment B, or vice versa.

In a basic way we can compare the artificial "Ice Walls" as a cell wall fulfills its function to act as a barrier that the, in this case, "pathogens" have to overcome to colonize that other environment or circle-environment, but it is also a dynamic structure, and then we could compare the Dome with a plasma membrane, in this way we could say that the wall of the Dome serves not only as a means of natural barrier of each "Circle-Environment" but also to restore itself in case of suffering any significant modification in its climate or general environment, separating the interior environment from the exterior, with exceptions in particular places.

We can call these channels "portals" or "passages" that help us to overcome these barriers that seem insurmountable, and generally are made by water, except for exceptions by technology that can be done through the air, but the passages both from the interior to the exterior and vice versa, are made by water as they provide a high percentage of success, as we were saying the domes are in the first instance as permeable "membranes" but sometimes selective as in the "Celestial Lands".

Although the domes are "natural" and are found, from the information we were able to collect, since the beginning of time, it is not ruled out that it was some creation prior to the beginning of the first colonizers, who were those who ventured out of their Dome or Membrane to explore other places, like a baby born out of the womb, civilizations have left their Domes to explore and exchange information in one way or another, Many of them still have not left by omission or ignorance, perhaps one goes hand in hand with the other, in our lands we humans have not left because of total manipulation of the colonizing parasites, otherwise I believe that today the same current civilization would be creating new ways to make way for what the extra-terrestrial destiny has in store for it.

To leave the dome then we could call it as the "birth of a race" in a certain moment or generation, the beginning to interact with other neighboring beings that surround, the colonizers thought that the "Great Dome" would work in the same way and that it would also connect to other domes and other lives, and that going out to the "outside" there would be another type of "birth" but none of this worked and all this remained as a big question mark, from there is also born the great doubt about what is found inside the "Celestial Lands" as mysterious as selective.

CHAPTER 9 - THE HIDDEN LANDS OF THE BOOK OF NINJ-MUH AND SHE-KI

There are several "continents" surrounding the First Walls, just outside the continents unknown to the seventh generation (or the great majority), and I say great majority because there is a small group of people close to secret organizations who are aware of this, as they have direct contact with some Custodians and who have served faithfully against our brothers.

These continents can be found under various names, and believe me, I have fervently read the thousands and thousands of books on maps and geography in general here in the Great Library of the Capital called "The Ark", and I have found the various lands that surround both yours and ours, and the names may be different and may be modified as they are studied, but, I have on more than one occasion asked many ancestral teachers, including Captain Butler, who has recommended to me one of the most complete and complex books of this beautiful culture, which could be called in the native language translation to something like "The Book of Ninj-Muh".

The people here are always willing to help in almost every task, but even more so if what one seeks is knowledge, being a bit of an attraction from the beginning of being a survivor who has crossed over from the "other side", that hostile place that today is looked at from afar, and having overcome a major battle here when the Custodians attacked us upon arrival, I think I have earned a bit of respect from the citizens and for that, they never ever reneged on spending hours sitting next to me to translate texts or help me understand the millions of questions and confusions I had in my mind, and still have, although a bit more dissipated.

The Book in question had very detailed maps and compared with the "Book of She-Ki", it was known that the giants had to their credit several and several of kilometers traveled under the Great Dome and were knowledgeable of both other worlds and other races, as they had been contacted and engaged in conversations with many of them.

It is worth mentioning the different existing Giant races, which are several, and not all of them are in favor of human liberation, although they are reluctant to discuss or explain in depth about this subject, what has reached my ears is that no Giant race would be against our liberation but simply many of them would not be willing to try to help us because of the consequences that this could entail, for example, what happened during the "Sixth Generation" with the Ancestors is reason enough not to set foot again on those lands that today are so far from my sight but not so far from my heart, my lands of origin, that I have called "Earth" so many times before knowing this path.

Following the Book of "Ninj-Muh" and comparing it with the Book of "She-Ki" we can come to the conclusion that, each race that lives in a land will name it in such a way that they can make themselves understood for their subsequent geographical location, tracking, and organization of the same, in turn in their native language or communication they have, consequently, the root of the original name of a site is always lost but rather begin to use others that are understandable and easy to locate based on the coordinates provided, there may also be some differences based on their actual location or shape as it was being done as technology and exploration were carried out, especially to the Second Walls and surrounding the "hidden lands" of Asgard.

From here I will humbly give you the names as they were translated from these books, but you can find several different names for each race, and if we consider the native language of the Ancestral Lands, then it would be even more complex that the translation does not lose the essence of each one, anyway I will try. (It should be noted that you will also find maps with different names within the "Known Lands" that will not have any relation with the names found in the Ancestral Library or that have been shared from here).

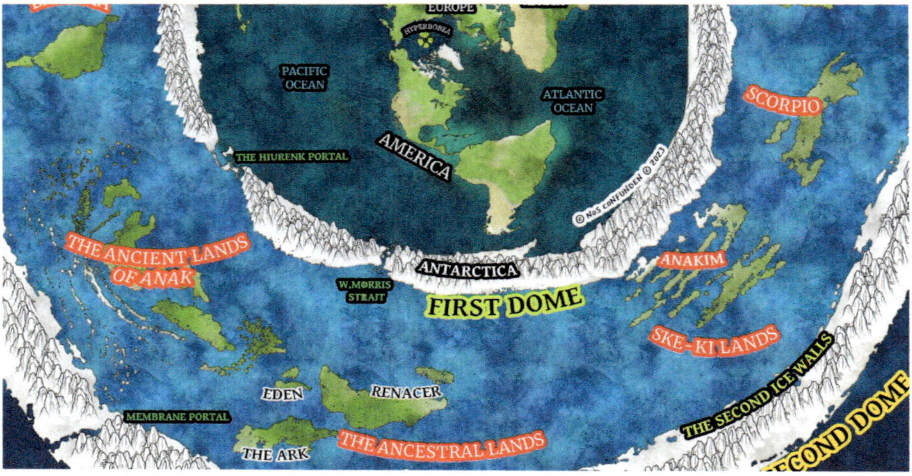

CHAPTER 10 - LANDS ACROSS THE ANTARCTIC POLAR CIRCLE

The lands where I am stepping at this moment, are called "Ancestral Lands" or "Lands of the Ancestors", they can also be known as "Ancestral Republic" or different names that sounded sometimes there in my lands of origin when infiltrating us with information.

In the Ancestral lands live mostly humans of the "Sixth

Generation" survivors of the Reset and the Great War fought there against the Anunnaki-Custodian power. Some of the survivors were able to regenerate their bodies in their entirety in order to reach the maximum possible life span (between the first and second dome) and lead a prosperous life continuing with other generations to come.

In these lands also live a small percentage of Giant-Humans, also survivors of the Great Tartary, and Giants of the South. Then a tiny portion is integrated by us, those who arrived during the "new humanity", some of the jokers here call us "the sleepers" as a way to differentiate them from the previous ones, since in the new humanity for the moment the vast majority do not know their essence and their environment, but as I said, it is just a joke because as in all resets humanity is born manipulated to not reach this information or make it covering as long as possible, possibly if there were survivors of past resets here they would call the next generation in the same way.

In this new humanity full of confusion and despair it seems to be simple to rewrite history and lead many down the path of spiritual self-destruction, once the majority does it, then it will only be time for others to imitate.

Today when the media is controlled, the interference is greater, I mean, the interference it will do in the minds will be to such a degree, as when one runs in terror before something or someone that gives us the feeling of imminent attack, it is not the same a state of alertness in mere silence than one being in a critical situation with danger of being attacked, you will get two totally different and opposite paths.

The Ancestors here are **81,039,041** people (at the moment I am writing this) that live throughout all these lands, although people do not crowd in the great Capital for work or to obtain another type of benefit as it happens in our lands, like any great city anyway it gathers a great number of people within the same number indicated.

There are some humans living in "The Ancient Lands of Anak" and in the "Lands of She-Ki", there are no records that there is another group of humans at least settled in other lands between the First and Second Dome that have at least sent signals or established some communication with these lands.

Crossing the Second Dome and Second Ice Wall and without any of the ancestral masters or She-Ki having confirmed it to me, it is said that there are humans in "The Lands of Venus" and that there is a great connection and relationship with the Venusians, in fact, when the parasites tried to colonize them, they were able to expel them by reaching an agreement, and within that agreement one of the strong points was nothing more and nothing less than the discussion about human liberation, although this was not achieved.

There are confirmed humans in "The Lands of Mars" from the known continents, many of them were sent there as a "prize" for having betrayed their own brothers, then this colony settled there along with other races. Some of the following generations have left these lands in search of another type of life, commenting that the life that takes place in Mars is totally conflictive and harmful in all its dimensions, a ship from there has arrived to our coasts as well as ancestral ones have infiltrated there by the "Byrd's Strait".

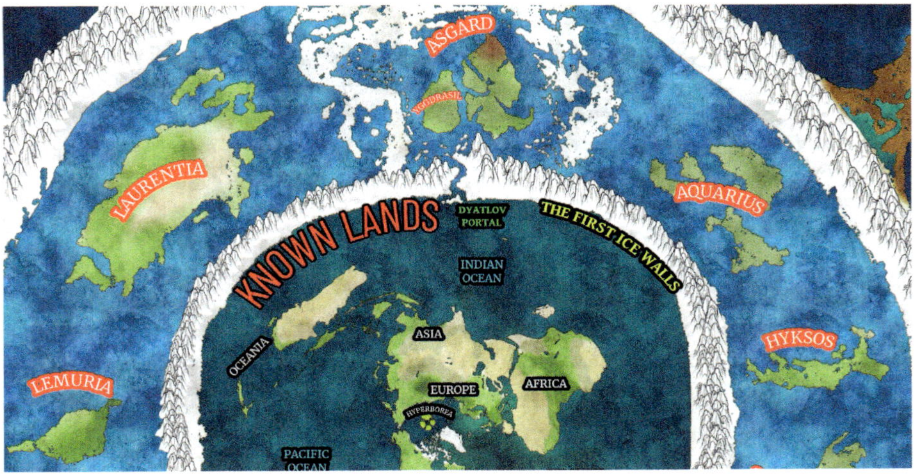

CHAPTER 11 - THE LANDS OF ASGARD AND THE DYATLOV PASSAGE

The "Dyatlov" passage has in its memories several remembered episodes and all of them were regrettable leaving only sad memories of the experiences. Reaching the gates of Asgard is not an easy task for almost any being, much less for humans, even worse if they are humans with basic technology that simply out of curiosity try it. In the ancestral knowledge it is known that there are several artificial portals created by the Anunnaki mostly, although the Custodians have also manipulated and used such technology for the transfer of matter.

Many of the portals were left in disuse and forgotten in different points of the many lands, the known continents are not the exception to the rule, and one of these portals is located in old settlements of the Great Tartary near the known "Ural Mountains".

Several explorers tried to reach it and use it to lead them directly to the gates of Asgard, almost always led by a person or leader who had come to the knowledge in some way, either by chance or some kind of information he could surely get from manipulative sources coming from "higher up".

For this reason, most of these expeditions failed and ended in a very bad way, one is well known in the use of this portal, they have a powerful scanner and this enables any custodian or force that is operating in the area to proceed even violently to prevent this from taking place, however, they are very unstable portals that were not stopped using for the transfer of material for their mistakes. Generally they are very old portals, but why were they not destroyed? This is the question I asked myself, the answer had several possibilities:

- **A** - They are not interested because the use of such a portal would lead to certain death.

- **B** - There is permanent custody in conjunction with high tech scanners.

- **C** - They are a trap for curious humans

- **D** - It is another form of Custodian-Anunnaki entertainment with humans (perhaps this option could come in conjunction with all the others above).

In fact, it is known that many of these leaders of direct explorations to hidden portals are often driven by the same Custodians who play with this human scouting group until they get there, even letting them cross the portal without really knowing what will happen to the matter they will end up moving, It is something extremely risky, but that the Custodians or other races, sometimes, with the desire to acquire energy from their fears or terror that they end up instilling, do not worry at all, but rather on the contrary, they end up taking advantage of it.

Be that as it may, these portals can still be found and are very dangerous, the "doors" of Asgard are not easily accessible and are hidden lands, so much so that they were used and thought to settle the first humans, knowing that they could be discovered but sought the best option to develop, the other lands they used are Lemuria to the East and Atlantis to the North, Asgard had direct connection through a portal with the lands called "Hyperborea" which are located in the center of the known continents.

In Asgard it is believed that there are still fortifications of the first humans and masters that gave rise to the great birth, but its access is complex as well as trying to pass through the passage "Bifröst" that leads to Atlantis and its neighboring land "Shastar".

The lands of Lemuria are today inhabited by a strange race of little development that was transferred from outside and that had throughout history very little contact with humans or Giants, there was found a long time ago very strange subway technology and of still unknown origin.

"Laurentia" on the other hand, is a land inhabited by Venusians, they are in this way the closest to our lands, it is believed that they send information to their lands of origin and leaders so that they are aware of all the movements and modifications that the colonizers make, it is expected that they can also come to help human liberation in the near future.

"Aquarius" and the lands of "Hyksos" are inhabited by hostile creatures in conjunction with the Lands of Sirens, there are several stories of humans who "collided" with these creatures that I will share in the next chapter.

In both the "Island of Death" and "The Lands of Death" there is no life, not even plant life, although it served as a passage for several races before penetrating the "Known Lands" today were simply abandoned. They are totally deserted places in contrast to their past.

In the lands of "Scorpio" there are three different types of Giant races, including the Anakim.

In the southernmost lands like "Argos" and "Athos" there were Anunnaki settlements, but today there is no confirmation of this, curiously it is dangerous to navigate in that area near the "Byrd Passage" and for that reason among others, it is complex to visit those distant lands outside the Second Dome.

In "Talos", lands near the Bridge of Hades, there is great darkness, the creatures that inhabit there are inferior of first generation without development, also transferred by the colonizing races.

In "Avalon" and "Anax" coexist two different races coming from outside, "Etamines" from Draco and "Grays" from Orion.

CHAPTER 12 - THE HUMANS WHO ARRIVED TO THE MERMAIDS LANDS

"History and Geomorphology of Adjacent Lands" - ARB201 - H101- Heimdall Bridge- Book of the Great Capital Ancestral Library "The Ark"

By the year 1900 of the last generation a ship had plans to visit the southern latitudes and explore an area that motivated many explorers of that time, without the Antarctic Treaty or the many maritime exclusions this old but resistant vessel headed straight to the cold Antarctic waters on September 28th.

Ernest, the captain, had an experience of almost 40 years, he knew every port and every corner, in the year 1923 he was sailing with ten other sailors over the famous "Drake Passage", the waves lashed the ship, they were intense swells that reached great heights, although the crew was really used to storms and complicated navigation, during the dark, lonely and gloomy night death seemed to call their fate on several occasions, there was no way to sleep a wink at that time.

To add drama to their then frustrated adventure, a great storm lashed the area and their boat became a simple paper boat sailing at the mercy of nature, the destiny was in the hands of what the "Earth-Mother" could decide before such a reality that struck full in their resistant and adventurous hearts. Everything was out of control for several hours that seemed eternal for those sailors, the course completely lost but not so the hope of each one of them who tried incessantly from one side to the other to keep the ship afloat, chaos and order from one second to another always played alternating for those times among all the old adventurous boats that were not content to travel the known, but rather to make way and history towards a new dawn.

Their old and wet clothes were not helping in the face of that raw cold that hit their faces, they now stood together as the rain and the waves seemed to give way, the hope that this generated ended up breaking in the face of that cruel and sudden winter that seemed to lash. Strange "Ice Walls" appeared before them, and they turned quickly so as not to break their ship into a thousand pieces before this sudden white wall, "majesty of the Gods" as they described it.

The deep Antarctic waters were wreaking havoc among the surviving sailors, so they began to sail in parallel and move far enough away to try not to die of hypothermia, although the impetuous swell increased its intensity as they moved away from that great icy wall. They began to observe that between this, until now, perfect and immense wall of ice, suddenly began to break completely at a vertex, not that the wall would fall before us, but rather as a large crack that generated an invitation to pass, who in their right mind would try with an old boat to dive into a suicide mission? Well, we would! But not because we really wanted to, but rather because we were slowly dying in the face of the painful cruel cold, the hunger and the totally unknown course.

Suddenly and without my being able to explain it in words, a great vortex seemed to emerge from the same sea, the swell did not intensify, but the vortex generated a strange swell that rotated like the hands of a great clock, first they went in the same direction and then in all of them in unison, we all became dizzy and we had to sit down or some of us directly fell on the wet and smooth floor of the boat, When I opened my eyes again I could see another vortex emerging directly between the crack of that Ice Wall, nothing seemed to make the slightest sense to us, I began to fear that I had died and that this was what they called "the beyond". Our bones that could hardly move because of the pain of intense cold suddenly began to obey the orders of my confused brain, the cold was not only gone, but there was no wall or waves hitting our hull, we looked at each other thinking the same thing, then we decided to externalize it with our vocal cords.

Where are we? Who could really explain this adventure? We were surrounded by a calm ocean, a reddish and strange huge dot, perhaps a nearby "Planet"? It appeared in the distance, compasses erratic, navigation problems continued, what other plan was there?

Simply to approach the only land that appeared on the horizon before everyone's eyes, would these lands be our true salvation? I think that before everything we had experienced and what we had gone through, and even without understanding how we had suddenly crossed some walls through two vortexes of light, the reality is that we were almost in agony between the storms, the intense cold and our ship close to sinking, we could call all this as a miracle and we could not see those lands as anything other than a salvation.

We arrived to its shores and we were beginning to doubt again how safe this area was, what other place was there? We all agreed on that answer, none, there was no more land in sight in an unknown sea, the question we all asked were we discovering new lands? And if so, where were we?

We descended, although some of the members did not want to, but our food and drinking water was scarce, we were in an absolute emergency, the sand was whitish and there was great vegetation in the distance, it gave a great appearance of being able to find fruits, rich and beautiful fruits! That's what I needed and urgently. We found some strange red fruits in some trees near the coast, we did not hesitate for a second to try them, we waited a while, perhaps not so prudent but we could not last much longer without food, we returned to the boat full of these red fruits in order to finish our provisions, which were not many.

It was nightfall in those lands, we were on the coast and there was no movement around, only the calm ocean generated some waves that kissed our ship that miraculously had survived. Although we were exhausted by all this mysterious adventure we could not sleep a wink yet, it was difficult to understand our position and even know what time we were in, we began to doubt again our reality around us, but we felt tired, pain, hunger, thirst and everything that a living human feels, we could not be dead and this was not at all what we knew as "promised lands".

Ernest! Ernest! They woke me up screaming, see that captain, what's that moving through the waves? Yellow lights seemed to illuminate our ship through the surface of the sea, a head appeared and shone directly in our faces, they are eyes! They all shouted as they hit our boat with force, the blows could be heard all around our ship. Because of the light they emanated and that reddish "planet" that illuminated the horizon I could make out their faces in more detail, they were eyes that emanated a strong yellow light, their faces were scaly and their untidy hair fell between holes that gave off water, they were the most terrifying beings I had ever seen, we all ran to our positions before my scream, and we were ready to escape from there immediately, they began to make deafening screams, they were communicating with each other or it was a warning to us, either one way or the other we hurried to get away from the area, these creatures sort of "sirens" of the most terrifying fiction stories remained in the distance staring at us as we moved away, their lights were lost in the horizon, the fear of the unknown is really paralyzing but this exceeded any expectation, we followed the opposite course to those islands but certainly aimlessly and lost in the strangest sea that anyone could have ever sailed.

We tried to find the location of where we thought we had arrived, and that strange vortex was there, but this time only one of them and in the horizontal part attached to the ocean itself, we stopped there and a white light emerged from the bottom generating the shadow of our boat towards the skies, seeing this suddenly we were again "on our side", but not near the ice walls but in the African coasts that three of us knew very well, the compasses began to work again, our destiny now was to go home and try to forget the strangest adventure we could have lived or expected to live, without a word to anyone about this matter or we would be locked up or accused of anything, no one would believe this experience.

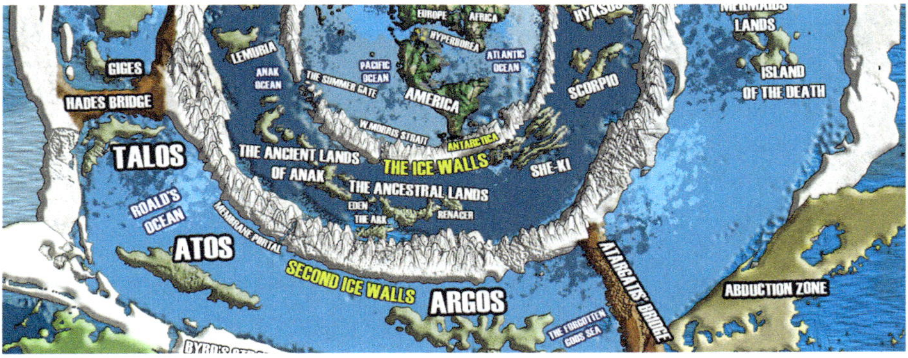

CHAPTER 13 - THE SECOND ICE WALLS

Another of my concerns when I found out about these second walls and understood a little of the functioning of the first ones, was the following: Why then are there ice walls imposed by the colonizers also here in this Circle-Environment?

Well, the answer I have received was that these lands when they were penetrated and taken in a violent and colonizing act by the Custodians, specifically after having failed in their visit to the neighboring lands "Venus" they took forward the creation of artificial walls so that information could not be easily passed from the core out, as they considered it of absolute weakness, it was sensitive information that the Venusians could use later.

The complex situation after taking these lands and finding the first humans developing, took place with several decisions along the history, and one of them would not be so long to wait with the creation of these walls that keep away in many ways any curious navigator that could try to cross the huge cold distances of the Second Ice Walls.

Anyway, this did not prevent that with the technology of the Giants one could cross to the lands of Argos or Atos or simply to the gates of the Mars Lands next to the "Byrd's Strait" who was recorded in previous books I have published, since Byrd himself was the one who would cross, "requested" at the time by the Custodians themselves and with their technology, helped by the Custodian Leader "Nimrod" who was later killed in a battle of the Ancestors near Lemuria.

So I don't think these walls were of much use to the coming generations (second generation onwards) since once they took control, humans could hardly have escaped from the First Dome. Crossing the "Second Dome" according to navigators and R. Byrd himself left a record of it, you feel a thrust and it seems to "sail through the sky" when you are penetrating The Ice Walls and Dome to "The Lands of Mars", the feeling could be described as being fired at an incredible speed and entering a deep abyss without having control for a few moments on the ship that is moving it.

CHAPTER 14 - THE STARS AND PLANETS IN THE HEAVENS, THE ABSOLUTE ZERO LINE CROSSING THE ANTARCTIC

This is another sensitive and not at all minor issue about how our environment works, the same conditioning can be "activated" as one tries to interpret the functioning and projection of the domes, the planets, the stars and the many worlds that seem to be far away from us "up there".

As Byrd and many other navigators who have been able to cross this passage leading into the interior of the "Lands of Mars" or misnamed "red-planet" have commented the thrust is similar, and it is important to remember this phrase once again, "As we navigate or traverse the very heavens" this could give us a closer explanation to what we understand as "Space" or "Universe" that in the science books of the "Known Lands" or "Earth" lead the new humanity to learn about reaching distant planets and stars as something extremely far away or even improbable by technology and studies, when in reality we can connect those planets or lands directly crossing these Domes in a horizontal way as directly crossing Antarctica or the Antarctic Circle.

Nowadays this is not possible for human civilians for several reasons, some of them we have already mentioned as the security guardianship with bases along the same circle, radars around the so called "South Pole", as well as the great distances of frozen oceans, huge walls and an extensive region of low temperatures without possessing adequate technology and the location of the passages already previously opened to find adequately and without errors the passage or portal to transfer matter from the interior to the exterior or vice versa.

Even with the right technology sometimes, as we will see later, mistakes are made that can end tragically, since the custodian technology advances and is updated frequently, for this reason only some beings are able to cross the domes, portals and even those Ice Walls that the custodians have left so that this impediment is increased to a maximum level.

But if all this were not already complex by itself, we also add what we know as a "strip" or "line of absolute zero" that is just before the First Dome, where events are experienced that we could consider strange or out of the ordinary, many space agencies and military of the new humanity study these areas periodically for many years, even many military have come to these areas to experience these phenomena (Byrd has also done so after his Antarctic expedition of 1934 in his experiment to spend months studying this famous "line of absolute zero").

This strange "Line" in addition to experiencing physical

changes, some people have visions of Polaris Auroras that plunge them to the most absolute depth losing track of time and their surroundings, visits from different times, coded messages that have reached them, images of deceased people that can appear before one, and a myriad of phenomena studied in depth previously by the Anakim, Ancestral and now a part of the new humanity with custodian complicity, make of all this phenomenon a place as recondite as strange, and as it could not be missing, the Custodians used this site to locate several humans and other beings to proceed to the study of war conflicts and psychological experimentation in these lands of the "absolute zero" (then you will find testimonies on this subject in later chapters).

It is very possible that this study is also related to the attempt to understand the connection of "The Source" that humans and the Celestial Lands (Terra-Incognita) have, since the entrance to those lands has always been the obsession of these beings (both Custodians and Anunnaki) since they first encountered them a long time ago.

ANTARCTICA SECRET MAP
MATTER LEAKS PASSAGE
THE ICEBRIDGE OPERATION
NASA
ABSOLUTE ZERO LINE
FIRST DOME
OUTER CIRCLE-ENVIRONMENT
× BYRD EXPEDITION 1934
TEMPORARY NAVAL BASE
UNITED STATES
SHIFTING LINE OF TIME CHANGE
THE BYRD CONFLICT
GREYS ZONE
ANTARCTICA
ICE WALLS
BASE 211
MAP BASED ON:
THE NAVIGATOR WHO CROSSED THE ICE WALLS: BEYOND THE ANTARCTICA
&
TERRA-INFINITA, EXTRATERRESTRIAL WORLDS AND THEIR CIVILIZATIONS
&
THE LANDS OF MARS: 178 WORLDS UNDER THE GREAT DOME

CHAPTER 15 - THE CONNECTION OF THE FROZEN WATERS AND THE CELESTIAL LANDS WE CALL THE UNIVERSE

As the title itself indicates: "The frozen waters can lead to another uncertain destination of those celestial lands that we call universe". It is difficult to understand this celestial connection between the existing domes and the stars or planets around us, when we advance horizontally through the portals we are connecting our matter and transport in a "natural" way towards the "beyond".

The "absolute zero line" is nothing more than a way of adapting our physical body and our conditioned mind to the possibility that these phenomena can be experienced, sometimes, many of these phenomena are presented to us, and very possibly after a strong shock, as well as other times they simply happen when we least expect them, we try to find then in our minds that are based on memories and therefore, on past experiences some kind of logic that can make us feel that we are not going crazy, but, many times it happens that along the time, we forget or even our own mind sends us messages that "none of that really happened" until we forget that event in a graduated way in order to continue with our daily "robotic" lives based on simple biological functions and competition among the same beings that this new humanity seems to lead in a frenetic way.

During the transit across "The line of Absolute Zero" we can experience the most sinister terrors as well as the most angelic songs that we have never heard before. The voices or images of those friends or relatives who are no longer with us, or the inner demons that will visit us before crashing into the First Dome, a shock of absolute reality towards the logic that we try to manage, a direct blow to the part of our mind that tries to control and pigeonhole everything. As if in a form of preparation for what is to come next, our mind must first walk through the inner hells before peering beyond our lands.

It is possible that this change is hardly noticeable if you have previously been able to break those chains that bound you to your past.

How then could we understand that the stars seen in the heavens are a mere specter of what we find around us through portals/passages?

The passages or portals that go through domes always connect with another reality, another time and another totally different atmosphere, both going and returning, when leaving a manipulated atmosphere as in the Known Lands the shock is even stronger, connecting with these hidden lands behind are simply a reception several times catalogued as "sacred" since in there you live a life with many unfounded fears and projected in your mind (of the new humanity) by the same conquering parasites that are above you or better said were placed there.

If you break this reality by going through a portal, you would be leaving the life you know totally behind, this does not mean that you will forget your past or your experience in the known continents, I assure you simply because I have not forgotten them, but it will change your way of thinking, not only by understanding a little better about how the plane you live and transit works, but that the Circle-Environment of your lands is submerged in negative energy and fears that infuse as part of their great food/pleasure the Custodians.

Then you will understand that the heavens are mere projections of a simulation that humanity lives daily even today within those lands that you inhabit, and that I have inhabited, like so many other ancestors, the manipulation that you live daily is simply sinister and it is something that we must break forever, not only those of us who are out here trying to help you, but yourselves, it is complex but not impossible when you can see what surrounds you, not only with your eyes, from a physical perception, but when all your energy accumulates towards the same direction in the mere silence, when there is nothing limiting and your connection is direct, you will be able to connect with other lands even without leaving the First Dome in a physical way, the celestial lands are also within you as "The Source" and the potential of your infinite spiritual growth that no other race here within this Great Dome possesses.

HELEN MORRIS, THE STORY OF THE NAVIGATOR'S DAUGHTER

CHAPTER 16 - A STRANGE VESSEL APPROACHES THE SHORES OF THE ANCESTRAL LANDS

Many of our books about the Other Worlds were interspersed with stories of our past heroes, both those who survived the Great War and those who fought and overcame the fear and uncertainty of what might really exist beyond.

The Anakim Giants would help to understand more about our plane thus adding to our Library a myriad of countless wisdom that was translated into the most sacred books and archived for further intrinsic study of what really surrounded us.

In time millions of reports, archives and texts were added that arrived from various parts of the Known Lands during and after the Great War, that the Giant-Humans knew how to obtain from many Custodian bases, until the time came to interrelate each point and each story that we received.

In this way we could reach many conclusions and knowledge that we did not have until then in the Ancestral Lands, We were able to identify many races and Circle-Environments that would have been impossible for us to elucidate by the mere fortuitous fact of how far our expedition technology reached, clearly we realized that our technology was not enough to make a great journey for the moment, besides first we had to investigate how much real distance existed and how many other races could receive us in one way or another.

The images of our heroes still shine among the great books, Captain Roald for example, who exposed himself to danger to obtain information from the Lands of Mars, crossing a passage little known at the time, and giving his life so that his companions could get out of there and tell of his exploits.

Many others sacrificed themselves so that our history and knowledge would continue to advance, and thus also, in addition to understanding these worlds around us, also reach the point of technology where we could go further advancing and be able to help the humans of our lands of origin, the point of being able to cut the "Resets" forever was undoubtedly one of the biggest reasons to be able to acquire more and more knowledge of our surroundings.

They were very complex missions and for this reason it was not very common to send men for the expedition crossing the Second Ice Walls, our knowledge was acquired in dribs and drabs, it was very slow and we needed to somehow understand much more about our environment inside the Great Dome. But without expecting it, one day our luck would change forever, this story has no waste and can also deliver several answers as it also converges somehow with all the information that we are delivering gradually.

One morning I awoke very early to strange murmurs coming

from outside my home near what we might call the "Main Port of Embarkation", my father William and Butler were also outside among the crowd shouting in excitement at something approaching us.

It was a clear morning so there was great visibility and about 500 meters from the coast a "coded ship" was approaching (Some advanced technology in some worlds allows to hide the real shape of the object and change it to a generic one or to one that "resembles the culture where it is approaching" but until then we did not know it) We saw it in black color without any distinction coming towards us at a great speed, I did not even have time to worry that it might attack us because William and Captain Butler were together with naval personnel very calmly waiting for this mysterious arrival.

This ship suddenly changed and adopted a very curious shape and even moved towards the inner part of the coast, our naval force was attentive but the silhouette showed a being waving towards our position without seeming to have any intention to attack, it was several seconds, but I think that inside me it lasted much longer than that, the tension when an unknown ship approached was always extreme as we had gone through several bad experiences in the near past.

It was difficult to distinguish what kind of being was visiting us, it should be clarified that we had received several beings from different parts of our plane, but this being did not match anything we had seen before, he came out with a smile waving from afar, the first thing he mentioned in a strange accent native to our Ancestral Lands, was that "his visit was going to be very brief and that he was passing through to other lands" as soon as he spoke with my father and Butler who accompanied him to the main building of the Naval Force to ask him some questions about his real purpose here, following the protocol, it was not a time to trust anyone, much less a being that we did not really know where he came from.

We feared he would be sent by the parasitic Custodian or Anunnaki races to really get some kind of information about our technology, numbers of citizens, military, or other kind of information.

The Being passed among the hundreds of people that we crowded there trying to get as close as possible to see both this strange vessel that practically ran aground on our shores and also this mysterious character of a bluish tone that was visiting us, his clothes were totally white, like ancient tunics that fell on his slender body, He was barefoot, his skull was disproportionately large and his huge eyes had a yellowish hue, he always kept a very strange smile since he descended from his big ship, he even looked from one side to the other as if he was grateful for the hospitality, I can not lie that he emanated vibes of great peace and confidence.

I wanted to go after my father, but William trying to protect me was reluctant to let me approach this new visitor, therefore, he strongly requested me to return home until I could talk to this visitor and be able to understand what he was doing there. Butler followed at his side at all times and never lost track of him, he was followed by several important members of the forces, as I said earlier, it was a day that would quite change the way I understood the plane we lived on.

I could never fight against my meddling ways, for that reason and since my father had not let me get close to this person, I slipped inside that big ship as I was not sure I would ever have a similar opportunity. This peculiar ship did not resemble anything we Ancestors had, nor anything I had been told about other worlds, we all claimed that it had changed shape between coming ashore until it finally ended up in the very sand.

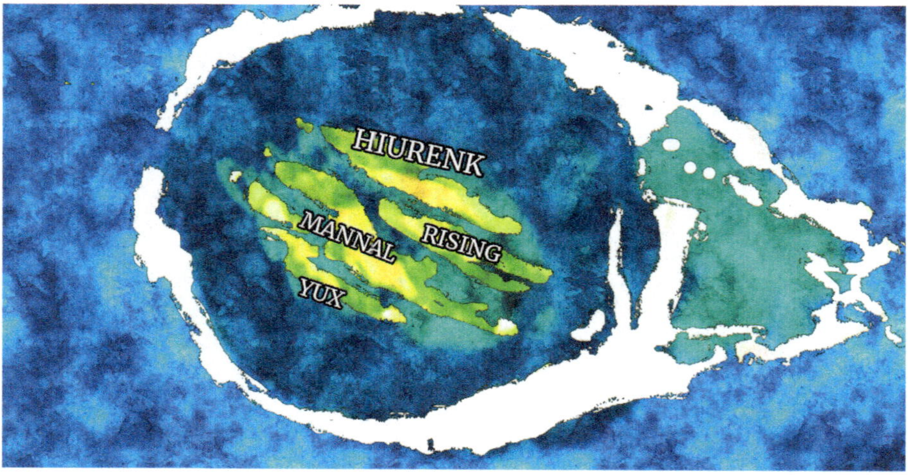

CHAPTER 17 - THE BEINGS OF CASSIOPEIA

As soon as I set foot on this strange boat, not to say the strangest that any human has ever seen, I realized for an instant that inside it was totally different, it seemed as if inside this ship was much bigger even than what it showed on the outside, but that thought fleetingly passed through my mind and evaporated from one moment to another when I found three beings in front of me, similar to the first one that had gone down with my father, they were staring at me.

Terror invaded my body and I was completely paralyzed, they

noticed it and quickly one of them advanced two steps towards my position and stretched his arm trying to somehow reassure me, or so I supposed, although by then I was terrified I felt inside me that they did not want to do me any harm.

I think I trusted more than I really should have, I always had these episodes that I called "ancestral-new humanity dichotomy", the part of my mother and my father, two generations that had merged and were now in me in some way.

While this could have gone really wrong and I might not be telling this whole story now, the truth is that the beings tried to calm me down and began among themselves to emit strange sounds while from their bodies emanated a bluish-white light, I did not fully understand what they were performing, but it was a kind of communication between them staring into each other's eyes.

This would be another strange occurrence but I was going to start getting used to all these experiences about the civilizations that inhabited under this Great Dome. One of them had a gray colored cube but then it would turn a pure reddish color and from this same object a kind of pale light would come out towards the wall and project an image, this projection on the wall showed without stopping one image after another of their Circle-Environment, their citizens, the way they lived, even the same Dome that enclosed their lands of origin, and to my surprise an image of what I interpreted would be of the confines of this Great Dome.

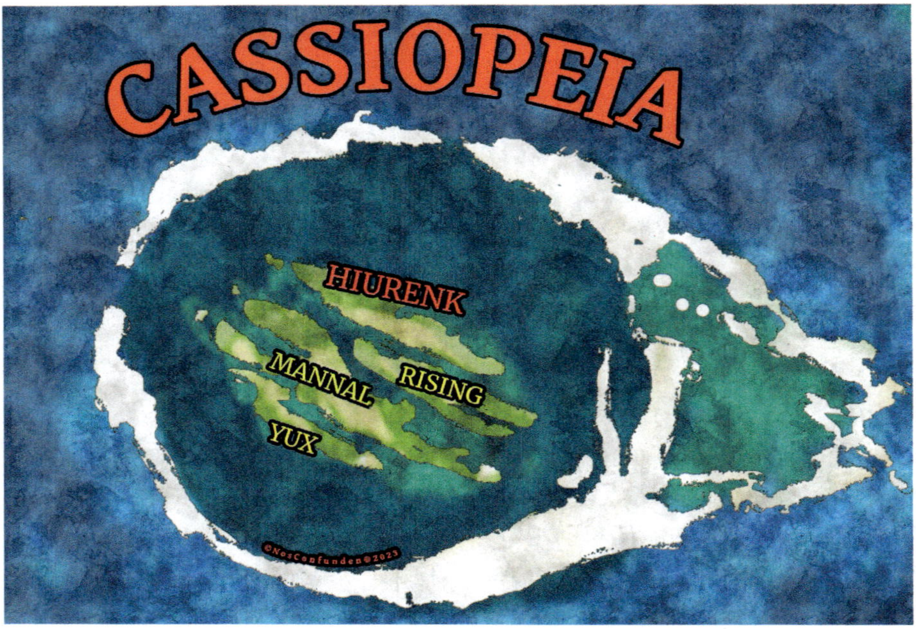
CASSIOPEIA
HIURENK
MANNAL
RISING
YUX
©NosConfunden©2023

CHAPTER 18 - THE BEING CALLED "HIURENK"

Between total astonishment and some frustration at not being able to initiate a conversation with these beings, I made signs to them so that we could leave the boat, to which they refused, I then assumed that they would not leave until their alleged "leader", who was meeting with my father and Butler, did not show up there to give some kind of indication or order.

While I didn't feel any kind of hostility or warning of danger in there, the reality was that I didn't feel comfortable either and even less so without being able to communicate with them other than with some signs where I felt like an infant trying to talk to the parents.

I proceeded to make signs of greeting and slowly retreated up a type of staircase that seemed holographic but firm enough to reach the deck.

When I set foot again on the shore and looked back again the boat had a different hue, more reddish, and it was not the product of our known Red Sun, however, the shape remained. Many citizens had seen me enter and approached me to ask me what was inside, I wanted to avoid any answer by making gestures of "not having seen anything", because if I commented that there were more beings, many other questions would not take long to arrive and it would be a long interrogation, there might even be some other curious person who would want to get inside.

My father was approaching in the distance with the new visitor and Butler and two marines followed him behind, they escorted him to the ship and I did not lose sight of them all the way keeping every detail. The being returned to the interior of the ship and now it was my turn to run to my father and although he was not going to be happy about it, tell him about the beings I had seen in there.

William was holding in his right hand the transcript of the whole conversation with the being, since every important event inside the big building is automatically transcribed, stored in memories and copies are generated, so that every answer can be analyzed in detail. My father was then very busy with other marines and chiefs of the different areas, therefore, I turned to Butler who with his distinguished kindness listened to my every word. Butler opened his eyes at every word of my story as he knew he had risked too much, but he was glad that I had been able to give him another piece of knowledge about these beings, then he told me that all this was somewhat similar to the version that the same being had given, and after my insistence, he promised to give me a memory to read the transcript of the visitor, who called himself "Hiurenk" and also like the rest of the team that came on the boat, they claimed to be from a place called "Cassiopeia".

CHAPTER 19 - THE PLAN TO RETURN TO THE LANDS OF ORIGIN

Everyone in the Ancestral Lands already knew my father well enough to know perfectly well that this welcome visit was excellent for our central plan of liberation of humanity, both the knowledge that these beings brought and their technology, especially the latter, and so my father would then try to make it all fit somehow into one of the plans they had created to return to the Known Lands.

In fact, I would later learn that he had not been able to resist too much and had proposed it to him in the first conversation in the Great Building. My father understood that time was getting tighter and tighter.

The transcript did not come to me from my dear father but from Butler, who had given me a copy of the hidden encoded memory. My father was trying to keep me away from all this conflict, but the reality was that we were all part of this long and arduous journey and, of course, I would be no exception.

Butler was confident, but from the expressions on his face, I knew it wasn't going to be easy to convince the new visitors to hand over valuable information about their technology, after all, we weren't sure they were aware of our origins and the visit seemed to be more casual than for some kind of mission or knowledge about us.

The night came abruptly before so much convulsion caused among the citizens, the news was not long in coming and spread all the information that strange beings had stopped on our shores. I noticed that my father had a great illusion for this new opportunity, you could see it clearly reflected in his face, I could never see him like that again and that filled me with hope at that time. I understood that inside him was the hope that "Hiurenk" would help to enter in a safe way to the home that everyone had had to abandon and somehow he dreamed that one of the many plans created would work for the human liberation inside the Ice Walls and the First Dome.

They were not so wrong based on the technology that these beings had reached and knew how to manipulate, in fact, I had seen it with my own eyes, the interior of that ship looked like something out of the best fiction books that my father talks so much about, our "Known Lands", added to their type of communication and the resounding change in the form that their ship could take, could be of great help in this way to slip away without any kind of mistake before the Custodian eyes.

CHAPTER 20 - THE TRANSCRIPTION

- Fhael: Well, it is a pleasure to greet you again, I introduce myself, I am Fhael, the president of these lands, on my right is our Commander in Chief Naval William Morris together with Captain Butler.

- Visitor: My respectful greetings, I am sorry for my accent, I will try to communicate as best as possible with you, please understand that my communication is visual-telepathic between our race, but we adapt well to the environment, and since this does not work with your race I will put all my effort in your type of communication.

- Fhael: Do not worry, again receiving you is a pleasant surprise, like most of every visit we have received here, we would like to know the reason for this and that you could give us more information about it since we are quite worried about what is happening in nearby lands and all our lands are on alert, where do you come from?

- Visitor: I am sorry for what is happening sir, my name is Hiurenk, our origin is distant lands called "Cassiopeia" or ARB032 we arrived to these lands sailing latitudes surrounding and somehow we have collided with your "Membrane-Dome" some time ago, we decided to avoid it until we met an extension in South direction, without remedy regarding our energy used by the vessel transporting us, having to penetrate the South Membrane-Dome of ARB204 (Mars Earths) avoiding ARB201 (Known Earths) for the time being, until we can better understand the functioning of its Circle-Environment in depth, besides the detection of our technology of what dwells there.

- Fhael: Sir, many points here are of interest to us, you comment that you have been able to penetrate the ARB204 Dome, has this required any difficulty based on your technology?

- Hiurenk: I am sorry I do not fully understand your question, but we have passed through that membrane without difficulty since it is at a level 2 with respect to our scale of 7. Therefore, I mean, we have passed through that barrier and then we have encountered "VStemcells" beings like you, but with different type of DNA, marking as a junction the type of origin detected.

- Morris: Hiurenk, have you been able to enter various Circle-Environments? -

- Hiurenk: That is correct, sir.

- Morris: How many of them have you been able to visit?

- Hiurenk: To be honest in our history not as many as other known races, but we have been able to go through enough of them to understand how many of them work, and many other beings that make up this Great Dome.

- Fhael: How many Circle-Environments do you consider to exist?

- Hiurenk: We have the information that there are 178 up to the giant dividing walls, but as I was telling you, we cannot confirm that since we have not been to each one, anyway, we have information on most of them that I will have no problem to give to you to add to your files.

- Butler: Excuse me, how has your experience been at ARB204?

- Hiurenk: One of the strangest, we have encountered various types of cells in there, and the control they have there is hostile, as well as among the beings themselves, we have seen situations of which we do not agree and do not accept in our civilization. We have also found experiments in laboratories under the surface, some abandoned and others currently in operation today, as I was saying, some are of the same species of origin, there is a group called "Human Colony" and within that strange Circle-Environment are the beings that value life above all others, but they are under constant attack, they have asked for our help and we have been able to free a contingent, but we have not wanted to participate actively since we try to stay away from the control in each Membrane-Dome.

- Fhael: Excuse me, Hiurenk, have you made contact with any of the races in control there? Rather, who are in control? And what kind of relationship do you have?

- Hiurenk: We are against any type of control over another being under any Dome, sir, we cannot confirm the race in control of ARB204 as there are several types in there, what we can intuit is that it could be undergoing some type of "control experiment" or other type that we are unaware of, no doubt it is an altered Membrane for the development of races of another origin.

- Morris: Have you been able to enter ARB201 (Known Lands)?

- Hiurenk: Negative, sir.

- Fhael: Forgive me for asking again, but your visit to these lands has not been clear, what is the purpose of your trip?

- Hiurenk: We have left our lands of origin relatively recently (depending on the comparison in each time-limit within the respective Domes), and are exploring lands for the knowledge and progress of our environment.

- Fhael: Were you under the control of some kind of species?

- Hiurenk: We have been under the hostile rule of the Custodians for a long time, clearly we had no possibility of growth or development of any kind, our race was just beginning to develop spiritually when it was colonized, many of our race have penetrated outside of our environment for fear that they would return, but the reality is that the Custodians left our lands long ago and we believe that they will not return, we also take this reason very important to be able to contact other races and to be able to deliver our small part of the history, if that can help in some way, although as I commented following our nature we cannot enter actively in any conflict of another species.

- Fhael: Perfect Mr. Hiurenk, for the moment I have no more questions to ask from my position know that you and your group are more than welcome to our lands, the Ancestral Lands and we will try to give you what you need to feel comfortable and you can leave whenever you want on your journey.

- Morris: I would like to be able to talk to you later about something very important, with Butler we believe that you could help us in our long fight against the Custodians, since you somehow were able to get rid of the colonization in your homelands, and we as you may know, are still in a battle that seems eternal.

- Hiurenk: Yes, I am very sorry for what happened in ARB201, it is known by many species around about your history, if in anything we can help know that you count on us, but we do not want to be involved in a direct conflict as that could endanger again my brothers in the lands we have left transitorily behind.

- Morris: I understand, do not worry, thank you very much for your time and I will be visiting you tomorrow morning so I can give you details and you can provide me with some information we need.

- Hiurenk: Perfect, I am here to help, grateful for your hospitality gentlemen.

CHAPTER 21 - THE NEW CASSIOPEIA TECHNOLOGY

That night my father would arrive again to the coast to meet that big boat that now had an opaque color and reflected the same sea that was hitting hard against it. With the help of Butler who told him about my contact with those beings in there, we were able to convince him that I also be part of this new contact, I understood later that my father also wanted me to witness such a conversation, as it was not going to be a regular one, but could mark a before and after in our development of the plan to free the new humanity.

We entered without problems going up to the deck and then descending by that "holographic" staircase that deposited us in a huge room, the dimensions did not make sense and seemed to be much larger inside than what we perceived from the outside.

Hiurenk approached us, he was alone and offered us something to drink, a drink of the strangest I would ever go to taste then commented that it was a fruit characteristic of his lands, it really did not taste bad but I was not used to it so I only tried a sip and left it there on a desk, I did not trust these beings much either, after all they were still a strange visitor (the drink kept its temperature from start to finish of the visit, and this lasted for hours, the container was a dark "gelatinous" cube that was very cold to the touch).

My father and Butler told him about the critical situation inside ARB201 and while they did not give any details of the plan, they needed to know more about both the enemy or enemies we were facing and also about the penetration of Membrane-Domes, as the latter was the most complex and where the Anakim Giants did not want to be an active part at the moment either. We thought that, if an outside race provided us with the necessary information to be able to enter undetected, we could also encourage the Anakim to join us in a mass release of new humans into our lands and surrounding lands.

This sounded far-fetched and unlikely, but hope was not lost, much less in my father, who had the illusion intact that these beings had arrived at the right time to somehow help us enter.

Hiurenk was honest with Morris and Butler, and told them that this could not be carried out as planned, but that they would give him information about technology to open a Portal/Passageway that could be at that moment above any kind of radar or custodian technology, that they had certainly done it on Mars Earths and that they had not had any problems.

My father was jumping with excitement, and I swear that if Hiurenk did not show seriousness as he seemed to be a being that would not show any kind of feeling towards us, my father would have given him the tightest hug at that instant. They agreed that they would travel near the First Dome - Ice Walls in a few days while they prepared their plan well, Hiurenk confirmed that he had the necessary technology to open a portal without being detected, but there was a primordial condition, Hiurenk commented that opening the portal would bring information to the new humanity about the spiritual development, and that was the only way to be able to free themselves from the Custodian/Anunnaki control, manipulation and yoke.

There was no possibility of winning any war against them at that time with the technology they carried, maybe some battle, but never a war inside a totally manipulated and controlled Dome and Environment, in fact, the humans themselves could turn against them with just some kind of manipulation of the means used there.

They agreed then that several ancestral masters would enter to provide information on spiritual liberation and development, the beings of Cassiopeia knew well that humans had infinite spiritual potential and that they were the "key" to the Celestial Lands, they were well aware that the Custodians were not going to leave the ARB201 colony easily as they had done in other Circle-Environments.

Hiurenk was also clear and concise about something, they would NOT enter into any conflict or help in any direct way, they would only open a portal with the guideline that information about human spiritual development would be entered.

CHAPTER 22 - THE HIURENK PORTAL, THE HUMAN SOUL, UNCONDITIONAL LOVE AND EMPATHY

So it was that during this "Silent War" between the Ancestors and the Custodians, the "First Operation Portal-Dome Breaker" was carried out, which consisted in melting ice, always taking into account statistics in order not to generate any climatic disaster, for a long time several ancestors departed from our ports to the "Known Lands" or "Ancient Lands" through this passage between fearsome giant icebergs, waves, and especially in front of the Custodian bewilderment, which when they discovered it already had several thousand of our masters publishing, teaching and prioritizing unconditional love and empathy as a way of life.

I must admit here that several people of the new humanity were rescued and left for our lands, but this happened in a small stage and with a small group.

The scientific conditioning almost collided abruptly by the time they realized what was happening in that remote area of the "Pacific Ocean", some 2000 ancestors were already scattered throughout the known lands delivering all information (some successfully and others not so much) about the infinite spiritual growth, questioning the scientific minds, what seemed unquestionable until that moment, that many secret organizations (with direct Custodian connection and manipulation) are made known and as if that were not enough, some human vessels arrived in the area by chance (and not so by chance) and left with great astonishment although only one of them dared to cross that dreaded passage, which was a death trap since it was not easily navigable, but would have to have great technology to cross it, but with a little luck, cunning and wind in favor, the impossible was forgotten when a group of five humans managed to cross it (It should be noted that this unfortunately was possible only in a short stage of weeks).

When the Custodians could notice that there was an ancestral hand in these teachings they tried to corrupt them, and they were easily annihilated, the spiritual path was manipulated in such a way that it was taken to dirty business, added to other repudiated subjects that together with the great media made that the great tower built on pure teachings was completely demolished in a few weeks.

Many masters were locked up and accused of different crimes, making known to all humanity the aberrant hidden causes they had, and somehow, they began to unite these noble causes with perversion, business and several other things that added to obscure the true purpose, some of them ended up in psychiatric centers at the mercy of "controversial behavioral treatments" in conjunction with experiments of all kinds that they carried out since then. Others were taken to prisons with the worst conditions, and others were killed outright.

The Custodians again went into a rage against their old enemies, the ancestral ones and the Anakim, for their most precious lands, they feared again an attack from us, in fact, when they found the passage we had opened with the help of the beings of Cassiopeia (Hiurenk Technology) they exploded and decided to attack our lands several times, but, they would do it in the most perverse way that they know how to do very well, then they granted very advanced technology for the time to the humans themselves, in that way the armed forces of the new humanity would attack several places before the "First Dome" but they would fail resoundingly.

The "Operation HighJump" of which we have already spoken previously was the scene that they expected to generate some fear in the Antarctic zone and to be able to militarize the zone, in this way they would also infiltrate custodian beings in some of the Antarctic bases and throughout the Antarctic circle to surround and undermine the zone with earthquake generating radars.

This type of technology generates earthquakes of great magnitude as soon as it receives an alert of infiltration of Ancestral Human DNA or some type of matter that they themselves previously added, this happened for a long time and continues to happen today.

Clearly this was not going to stop my father Morris and Butler to continue on their way to achieve the liberation of the new humanity, they would look for other ways and no doubt they would dare to infiltrate again in the lands of origin, Hiurenk had given them some information to penetrate the Membrane by air, but it was a very risky mission, although as I said, greater was their illusion to liberate them.

CHAPTER 23 - THE 178 KNOWN WORLDS

Hiurenk before leaving again to "Cassiopeia" lands, or at least that was what he told us, gave us several memories to file in our "Great Ancestral Library" about the other worlds that they had been able to know and others that they had not entered or perhaps not even navigated closely but that they had acquired from several other races and from books as old as the beginning of life itself.

We in the Ancestral Lands compiled all this information and after extensive and arduous work of managing, comparing and gathering all the works, reports, reports and texts, we have come to the conclusion that these are all the Worlds (Circle-Environments) that lie beneath the Great Dome, or within the vast and enormous walls that contain and divide the known from the unknown.

ARB201 KNOWN LANDS - EARTH
ARB204 MARS
ARB123 VENUS
ARB013 ANUNNAKI
ARB004 PLEIADES
ARB206 SATURN
ARB207 ALDEBARAN
ARB208 ANGELS
ARB210 PEGASUS

ARB032 CASSIOPEIA
H005 ORION
X001 CUSTODIANS
X003 JUPITER
C412 HERCULES
C413 ANDROMEDA
C414 ARCTURUS
C415 VANTH
C416 BETA LYRAE
C417 SAGITTA
C418 SHAM
C419 VEGA
N820 SADALMELIK
N821 SADALTAGER
C422 MIRFAK
C423 ALGOL
C424 MENCHIB
C425 SIRIO A
C426 NUCLEUS 270
N827 ALTAIR
N828 SIRIO B
N829 ALFA CYGNI
N830 NML CYGNI
N831 P CYGNI
N832 SADR
N833 CYCLOPS
N834 FAWARIS
N835 ALJANAH
N836 EFIALTES
N837 WR 142
N838 HYDOR
N839 SADALSUUD
N840 CLOUD LANDS
N841 NUCLEUS 290
N842 16 CYGNI
N843 ELENEI

N844 ALBIREO
N845 DAMASEN
N846 PERSEI
N847 ATIK
N848 GORGONEA TERTIA
N849 GORGONEA QUARTA
N850 NUCLEUS 272
N851 ETERNAL
N852 MIMAS
N853 DRACO
N854 DELTA 2 LYRAE
N855 QUAOAR-X
Y556 NEPTUNE
Y557 LANDS OF CLONES / SECOND EARTH
Y558 URANUS
Y559 LEONIS
Y560 TITANIDES
Y561 TIERRA CEO
Y562 FOUNDER LANDS
Y563 NUCLEUS 286
Y564 DENÉBOLA
Y565 TRANSMUTE
Y566 CRONOS
Y567 PAN
X068 BALDER
X069 HEL
X070 TYR
X071 IDUNA
X072 CALIGULA
X073 THE FINAL DOME
X002 NIBIRU
X075 HEIMDALL
X076 GREEN STONES
X077 ARA
C478 AQUILA
C479 SCUTUM

C480 CORVUS
X081 PLANET-X
C482 ALGENIB
C483 MARKAB
C484 HELVETIOS
C485 ENIF
C486 LANDS OF TIME
C487 ARCANE ISLANDS
C488 CRUX
C489 FROZEN LANDS
C490 DIMIRIO
X091 INFINITE LANDS
C492 BIHAM
C493 HOMAM
C494 EL TEMPLO DE ZEUS
C495 CELESTIAL RINGS
C496 ROSS
C497 MATAR
C498 SALM
C499 SCHEAT
C4100 VERITATE
C4101 TITAWIN
C4102 CRATER 18
C4103 DELTA 1
C4104 STEPHENSON 1
C4105 R LYRAE
C4106 XY LYRAE
C4107 MERU
C4108 POLIBOTES
C4109 ORIOS
C4110 CLITIO
N8111 ARTEMISA
N8112 PERIBEA
N8113 SKAT
N8114 POLO
N8115 EDASICH

N8116 RASTABAN
N8117 MERCURY
N8118 MAIA
N8119 THUBAN
N8120 NOVA PERSEI
N8121 DÁNAE
N8122 U SAGITTAE
K001 CELESTIAL LANDS / TERRA-INCÓGNITA
N8125 LACERTHA'S LANDS
N8126 BABCOCK
N8127 BACO
N8128 HYDRA
N8129 ERIS
N8130 ALKAID
N8131 NUCLEUS 284
N8132 TANIA AUSTRALIS
N8133 EOLO
N8134 BOL
N8135 LANDS OF THE STORMS
N8136 ETHERNAL FIRE
N8137 ALCOR
N8138 MIZAR
N8139 DUBHE
N8140 KURHAH
N8141 RAI
N8142 LANDS OF THE FORGOTTEN HUMANS
N8143 SKADE
N8144 NUCLEUS 294
N8145 BÓREAS
N8146 CIH
N8147 NUCLEUS 282
N8148 ERRAI
N8149 PHICARES
N8150 TSAO FU
N8151 SCHEDAR
N8152 ALFIRK

N8153 SEGIN
N8154 RUCHBAB
N8155 CAPH
N8156 SOUND
N8157 TASO
N8158 NUCLEUS 276
N8159 ROTANEV II
N8160 SUALOCIN
N8161 MUSIC
N8162 ALDULFIN
N8163 WASP
N8164 ORO
N8165 POLUX
N8166 LANDS OF THE SILENCE
N8167 CASTOR
N8168 ALHENA
N8169 SHERATAN
N8170 ARIETIS
N8171 NUCLEUS 274
N8172 TOXIC LANDS
N8173 BRAHMA
N8174 NUCLEUS 280
N8175 MEKBUDA
X176 ADDU
N5177 WISE
N5178 GIANFAR

THEORY-BASED MAP OF OTHER SURROUNDING DOMES

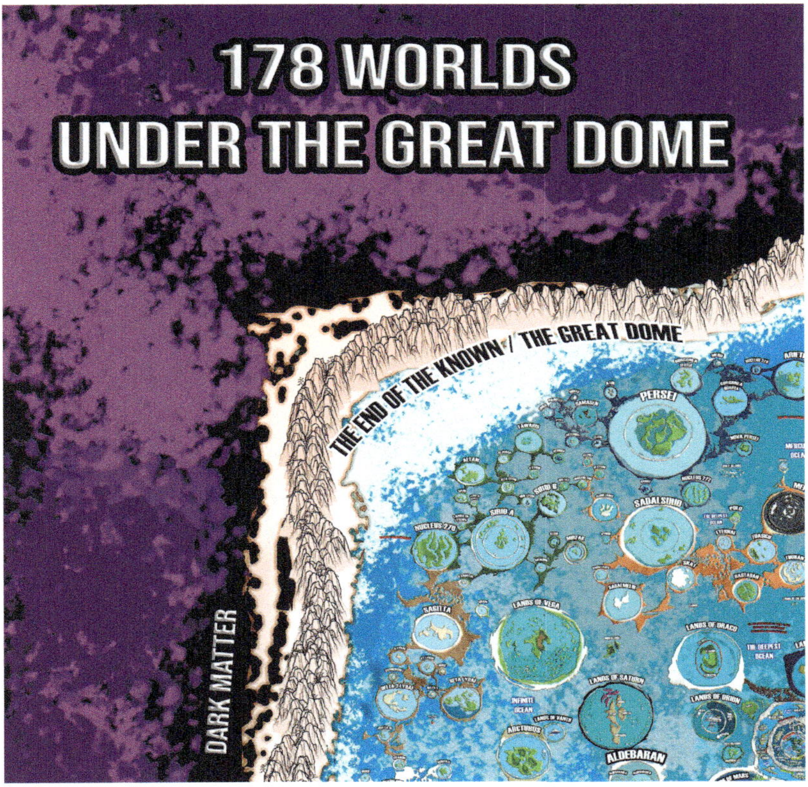

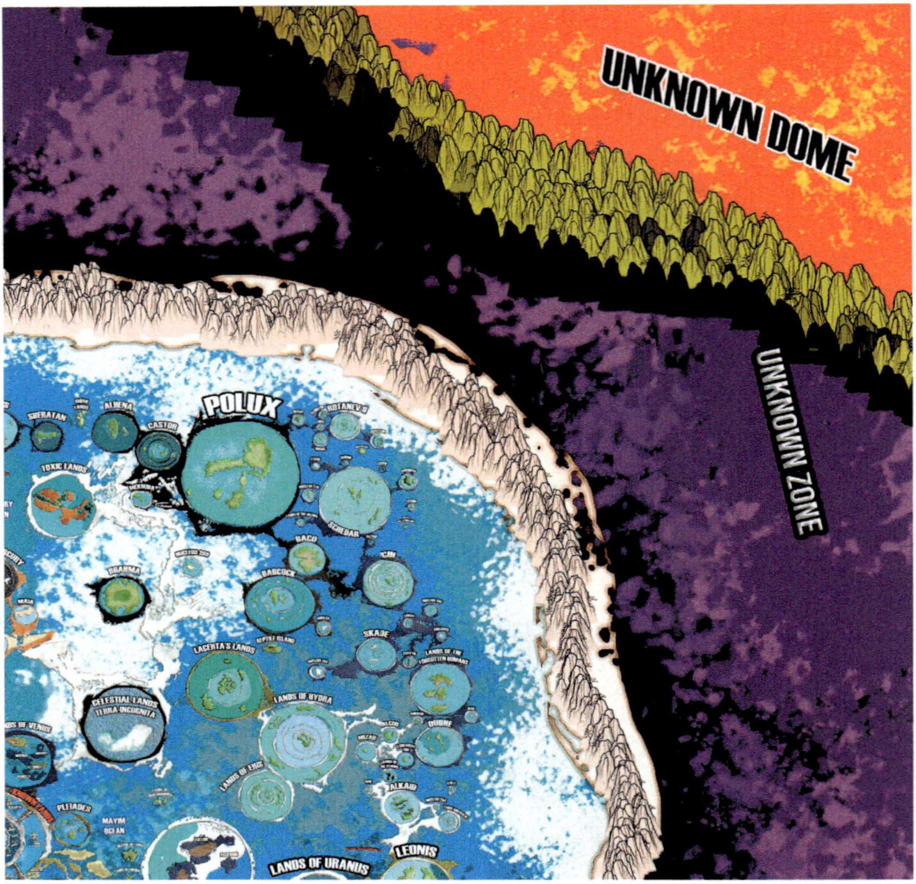
UNKNOWN DOME
UNKNOWN ZONE
SHERATAN
ALHENA
POLUX
ROTANEV II
CASTOR
TOXIC LANDS
SCHEDAR
BACO
CIH
BRAHMA
BABCOCK
MAJA
SKADE
REPTILE ISLAND
LACERTA'S LANDS
LANDS OF THE
FORGOTTEN HUMANS
LANDS OF HYDRA
CELESTIAL LANDS
TERRA INCOGNITA
DUBHE
LANDS OF ERIS
ALKAID
PLEIADES
MAYIM
OCEAN
LEONIS
LANDS OF URANUS

ANDROMEDA
LANDS OF ANGELS
CASSIOPEIA
PEGASUS
LANDS OF JUPITER
TITANS
OCEAN
LANDS OF HERCULES
AQUILA
NIBIRU
UNKNOWN ZONE
COPYRIGHT © NOS CONFUNDEN © CLAUDIO NOCELLI

ANUNNAKI'S LANDS
LANDS OF NEPTUNE
SECOND EARTH
LANDS OF CLONES
LANDS OF QUAOAR
LANDS OF TYR
BALDER
PAN
DARK MATTER
THE GREAT DOME
UNKNOWN DOME

TERRA-INFINITA MAP WITH NAMES APPROPRIATE TO THE NEW GENERATION

TERRA-INFINITA MAP

CODIFICATION

WORLDS DIVIDED INTO PARTS ACCORDING TO

"N-X ZONE" CODING

WORLDS DIVIDED INTO PARTS ACCORDING TO "C-X ZONE" CODING

WORLDS DIVIDED INTO PARTS ACCORDING TO "ARB-X ZONE" CODING

WORLDS DIVIDED INTO PARTS ACCORDING TO "X-X ZONE" CODING

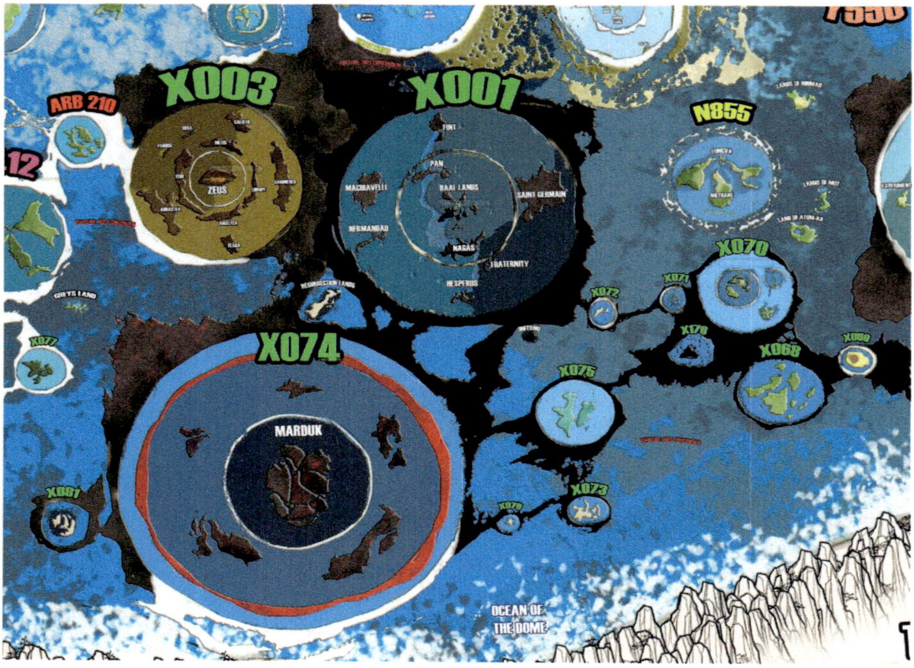

MAP DIVIDED INTO PARTS ACCORDING TO SPECIAL CODING:

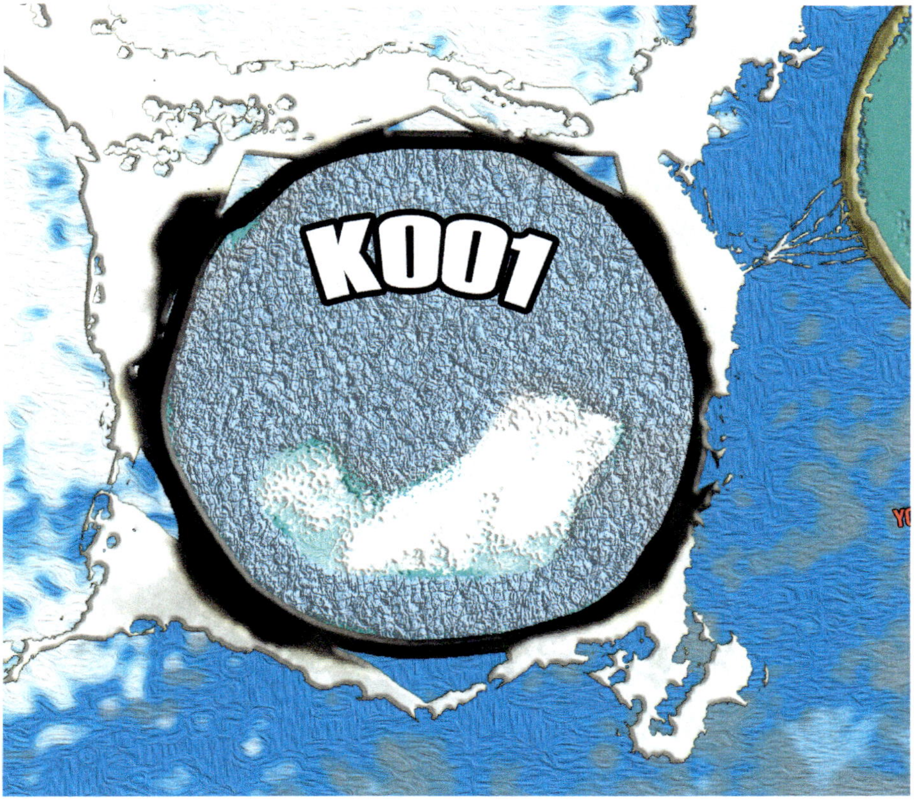

WORLDS DIVIDED INTO PARTS ACCORDING TO "Y-X ZONE" CODING

STORIES OF THE PLANET-WORLDS INSIDE THE GREAT DOME

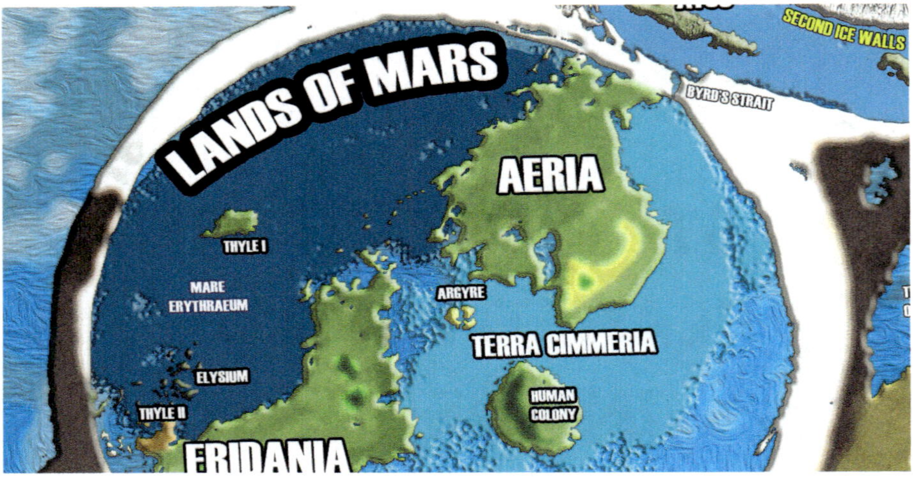

ARB204 – THE LANDS OF MARS

What we know about their civilization of origin: Killed in war against colonizers, it is believed that some of them managed to survive and emigrate from their lands, but there is a lack of information to confirm it, it was believed that the "Martians" had been annihilated in their entirety, but, the most recent theories speak that a not so numerous group could be living on the coasts of nearby lands and that they had been sighted by several races.

Their present: The lands are occupied today by different types of races, including the human race ("VStemcell"), it is a zone of controlled development, there are conflicts and wars of all kinds.

We have information that a part of the human race living there in a large colony migrated to other lands that have visited ours in past times. Also some of our navigators have penetrated its passage/portal to the interior and have informed us in detail about some of the species that live there.

They are lands of constant conflict between many of the races that inhabit there (especially the one coming from The Lands of Orion - H1ORION -) and little or no spiritual growth, it is believed that the various races compete with each other in the development of weaponry for defense and attack.

Many humans arrived from the Known Lands as a "reward" for betraying their own race, this was happening also during the period that is today the last "post reset" humanity, as we were able to gather from several navigators who went into the connecting passage between Mars and Second Dome Lands we were able to obtain much valuable information regarding how the Human Colony lives there after years of having left their homelands.

All the members who arrived there as a "prize" did it with absolute happiness imagining that they would live in a paradise and that they would live five times more approximately than their current average life on the known continents because of all the existing polluted and manipulated environment.

But, when they arrived they realized that the Custodians had betrayed them in a certain way and that all their help and betrayal to their brothers had been just another trick that the Custodians used to perform. They would manage to live much longer (if they survived the many current wars) but they would do it in a really different way than planned or promised, as long as their bodies could be absolutely "cleansed" of the manipulated environment of the old and known lands.

Although the lands of Mars have paradisiacal coasts as well as an incredible variety of flora and fauna, the variety of colors in each landscape is really catching, but, the wars that are carried out by the many races that coexist there make of these lands a true hell.

Both Captain Hunt and Roald and so many others, who are proudly remembered as examples every day in our lands since they helped enormously to gather information to understand our environment, told and detailed their experiences in these lands penetrating the well-known "Byrd's Passage" and all that was also of course as proof of fire kept in our memories of the Great Library.

The writings of Captain Hunt are quite consistent with the other accounts, the "Human Colony" existing in the misnamed "Red Lands" began first on the shores of Aeria, and then forced by other races, especially the harassment they received from the Grey Race of Orion (H1ORION) in conjunction with the "Etamins" from the Draco Lands, led the human group to settle on a large island off its shores, in Terra Cimmeria. At the beginning it was hard work to build their bases from scratch again, but they had custodian technology that had been given to them upon entry (possibly as a modality for all races in this experiment), so it was not so difficult to make their dome-bases operational again. The buildings in the Mars Lands were "Dome" or "Dome" shaped and it could not be otherwise since it had been imposed also by the Custodians, among many other requirements to live there.

Humanity suffered from the beginning and then it was not so

different, the attacks of the Greys and Etamins had ceased in intensity, but not radically, every now and then they received attacks from the coasts and these missiles impacted near the operational bases and had even affected several domes created by the humans, generating many casualties.

One morning the Greys attacked their coasts directly and killed more than 100 humans who were not prepared for a confrontation, it was really a massacre and this was told by a direct witness in the visit of Captain Hunt. The brave navigator had left our lands in the direction of the Ice Walls - Second Dome in order to face the dreaded "Byrd Passage", since it was said that it was a passage/portal that was very complex to go through, besides the experience could be really traumatic.

This was not an impediment for Hunt and his crew, in total there were 8 people who left in a ship in the direction of the "Membrane Portal" and then to its passage through the "Roald's Ocean" in a West-South direction, between the Lands of Argos. The passage or Membrane Portal (crossing the Second Dome) is a very complex site since very few ancestral explorers have dared to cross it, although the "Anakim" Giants have helped us a lot to get through, the reality is that it is still unstable for us and we try to avoid it, not only because of its difficulty but also because of the length of the route. Captain Hunt and his men left armed structures on the shores of Argos, in case they needed to return urgently, as well as to help the next visitors who wanted to risk entering through Byrd's Portal.

The ancestral technology could safely detect, or so we assumed at the time, any enemy approach, whether from the Greys, Etamins or any other race, except the Custodian, for that reason it was extremely risky to navigate in those latitudes. In any case, it was a risk we wanted to take if we wanted to bring back information from those lands that could be of great use for the human future both within the first and the second dome. We were not yet aware of how the humans there would react, although we knew about the existence of a colony and we had had contact with a boat that had escaped from there, a possible confrontation against them was totally uncertain, but as we said, we had to try, since those humans had direct contact with the Custodians and although we had a totally negative view towards them for having betrayed their own race, the information there was as valuable as gold in the known lands. Besides, we wanted to know how they had developed there, if there were still wars, or even worse, if there was still a human being in there.

The first encounter took place exactly 17 days after crossing the passage/portal, which, as a side note, was not so traumatic to go through, but Hunt records a sensation of being pushed at breakneck speed for a few seconds and upon entering you totally lose control of the ship, added to the fact that the radars stop working for a long time and the sensation of having been inside that passage for a long time, all this was really catastrophic for people like us who were entering hostile zones and had no way of knowing where we were navigating or if there were enemies nearby.

It was not until five days later that we were able to recover our technology and get it operational again, and when everything was fully operational, we decided to set sail along the coast of Aeria. Then Hunt tells in his memoirs: "The sea off the coast of Aeria is one of the most incredible that we had ever sailed, from afar everything seems peaceful but there is a swell that from nowhere becomes a thrust so violent that the direction is completely lost, as close to the Walls of the First Dome, our boat was prepared but the swings made some of us ended up sick for some time.

We tried to reach "Argyre" that from its distant brightness dazzled our senses, we were called and attracted there as the ancient stories of the Siren Lands tell, only the sunset, the violent sea and us, the stillness suddenly invaded us, all was silence for some time until we touched the shores of Terra Cimmeria, it was time then to face reality, it was all or nothing and my men knew it very well, would there have been any human left standing there? And if so, how would they receive us?"

On those shores there were three humans doing some kind of repair on the dock that from afar marked somehow, that there was a large human settlement there. We approached with our boat very slowly, the moment of tension increasing as we passed. Because of our type of boat they surely had no idea who we were, and this worsened the conditions to establish some kind of signal before contact. Our entire boat was illuminated with white from end to end, the message was clear, we did not want to initiate this contact in the worst way, nor that they interpret any kind of hostility, after all and even if we were so far away in our ideals, we were human beings in unknown lands and far from our origin.

On the shore the humans now "Martians" had stopped all the activity they were doing and were staring at us from there, each one in their position far away from each other by great distances, this caught our attention, usually in an arrival in this way those who receive visitors are grouped and try to welcome or not, but the ways were different from what we thought.

Our ship parked close to the shore, the sea in that area was extremely deep, and I descended with my companion Richard, who was the most diplomatic, to make known the purpose of our visit.

Richard made signs before descending towards the base that would transport us to the same white sand of Cimmeria, the humans there saw us from afar without making any movement, they did not even talk to each other, they seemed robotic actions.

They were very young people in appearance, and their clothes were dirty and torn by the hard work under the Martian sun.

A man came towards us and greeted us cordially, he told us that it had been a long time since he had heard an accent like that, strangely what we least imagined but most wanted happened, it was a cordial welcome from the human colony in these lands of suffocating heat but beautiful scenery. He told us that they called him RS200 and that all of them had names like that, between letters and numbers to differentiate themselves, and that long ago the proper names had ceased to exist there, Richard asked him about Byrd and other known names that we knew had entered these lands long ago, but neither RS200 nor the others knew how to give us information (or did not want to).

Later Richard would show him a picture of Byrd that some people knew, their answers were confusing and ended up saying that "R. Byrd had left the lands long ago. Byrd had left the lands some time ago" but we don't know if they were referring to a death or that he had physically left the shores, we didn't want to insist for the moment, although we wanted to know his whereabouts.

First of all, we asked him about the Custodians and leaders there, these young men were exactly 26 people living together in pitiful conditions and seemed to have been abandoned, although later we would learn of something worse than this.

The leaders were called "Cuijas" and we were told that they approached them in particular ships, silent and that "walked the waters", these beings had clothes that simulated or rather, that were shaped like animals known from the area of Terra Cimmeria.

To use this type of costumes was quite common among the Custodians, when they approach beings of their Colonies, we suppose that it is to confuse both the same beings and the histories that they can leave towards the future, we can find it in thousands of representations within the Known Lands, for example, in the Ancient Egypt of past generations.

The "Cuijas" as they called them, did not often come there, but they had certainly been moved from one zone to the other, the island was well divided into four parts, and the zone we had arrived at was a "Zone of Reclusion" or "Zone of Punishment", where for some reason they considered that they had violated some established rule, they were taken there as a punishment performing subhuman labor in high temperatures under the sun, with basic tools, for this reason they had received us in this way, they were not even surprised, I guess they imagined that it was another mental game of the Custodians and part of their punishment, or perhaps they were begging for some kind of rescue to come from outside.

Very curious all this experience, the first humans arrived to these lands with the promise from the Custodians to live in a paradise for more than 500 years, and they found this reality where they, their children and probably several future generations would live in pitiful conditions.

This all seemed like some sort of divine punishment for betraying humanity, but the reality was, the Custodians and

Anunnaki themselves were playing with human minds no matter what rank or closeness they held.

Both Hunt and all the crew, after talking and spending two nights there in this area considered as punishment, moved away from the coasts trying in a very risky way and out of the plan, to reach Eridania, they had obtained some important information about this area and they did not want to lose the opportunity to visit it. If they were detected by some Custodian radar, approaching a portal or Anunnaki Pyramid, or simply some other race that could alert the presence of ancestors there, the whole Circle-Environment would go into alarm and the impossible would be done to find them, for that reason to continue sailing there after so many days, knowing that at least another three days would be needed to return to the Byrd Passage.

It should be clarified that the humans in the "confinement zone" begged on several occasions to take them out of there, they flatly refused, not because they did not want to help them (after all they were a new generation paying for past mistakes) but because taking them near Byrd Passage or navigating through its seas could be easily detected, since the "RS2XX" carried several tracking chips with custodian technology very difficult to manipulate, they had neither the tools nor the laboratory, nor the suitable personnel to perform a surgical extraction of that technology in their bodies and/or blood.

Since they could not contact any ancestral base, not even the structure that could detect the signal left at the gates of Mars, since any attempt could be detected there, the risk was even greater, first that they could not be rescued and second that if they were captured or killed the complete information would be lost and all the answers that the human prisoners of Cimmeria had given them about their entire colony would have disappeared completely and the entire trip would end without fulfilling its main objective, besides not having been added to the memories of the Great Library.

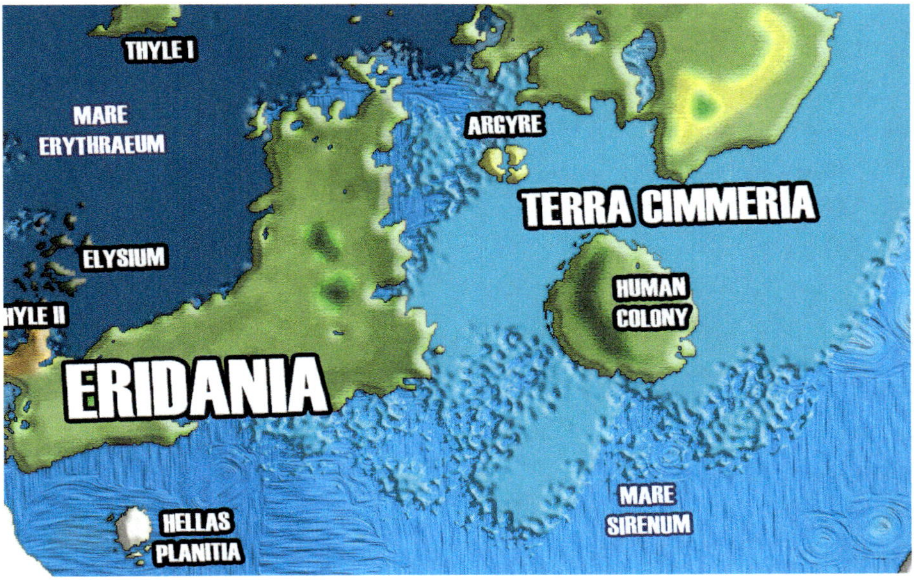

When they were on their way south towards the lands called "Eridania" the distances were extremely large and the "Mare Sirenum" became even more and more dangerous as it passed, the technology of the ship was not the best, so we decided to return immediately. Surprisingly all the crew arrived correctly and without conflict against the Custodians, Anunnaki, Greys, Etamins or any other race, and the information gathered by the humans there was really valuable, after overcoming the passage of Byrd from inside to outside, the entrance again to the Known Lands of the second dome was a relief, three days of rest, Three days of rest, contact with base, transfer of files and internal rejoicing for having complied, we now undertook our return to the Ancestral Lands to tell from our own mouths to the thousands of impatient souls who were waiting for us, leaving us with a strange sensation on our return, had the Mars Lands been or were being somehow abandoned by the colonizers?

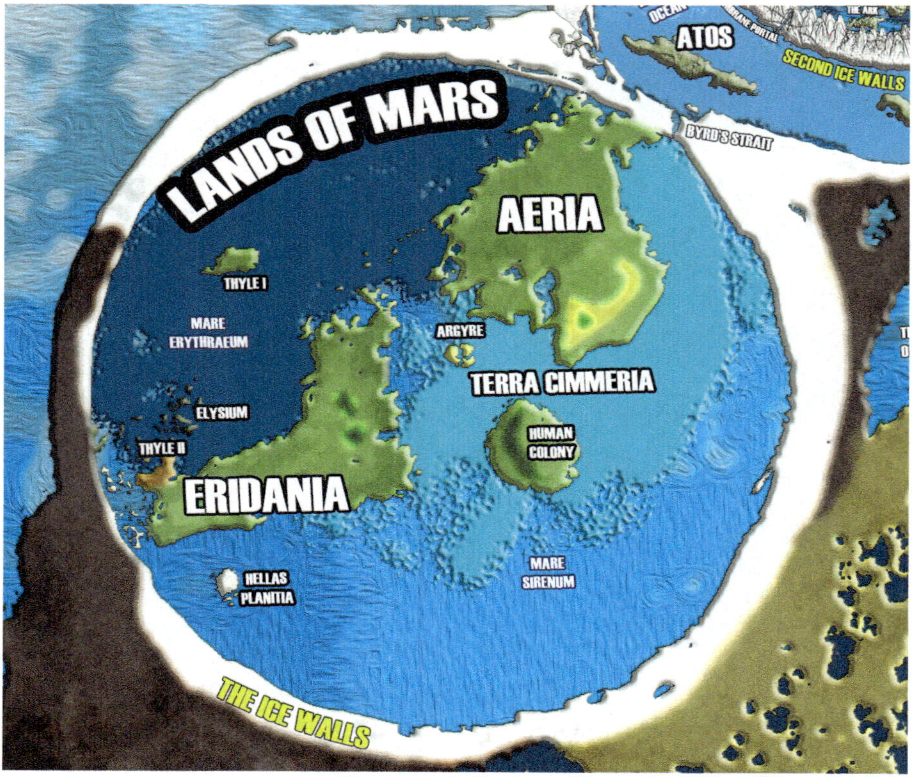
LANDS OF MARS
ATOS
SECOND ICE WALLS
BYRD'S STRAIT
AERIA
THYLE I
MARE
ERYTHRAEUM
ARGYRE
TERRA CIMMERIA
ELYSIUM
HUMAN
COLONY
THYLE II
ERIDANIA
MARE
SIRENUM
HELLAS
PLANITIA
THE ICE WALLS

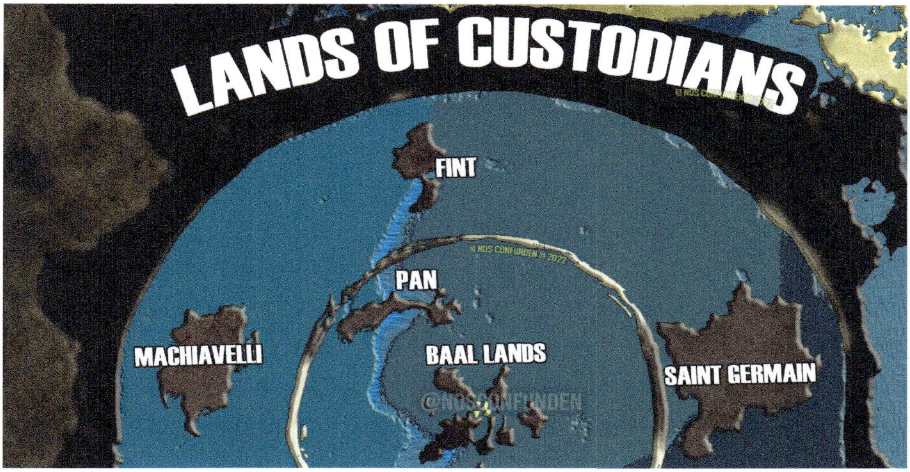

X001 – THE LANDS OF CUSTODIANS

Inhabitants (Approximate Data): We do not have an exact figure, it is believed that more than 27,000,000,000 and others scattered throughout the plane in their Colonies within the Great Dome.

What we know about their civilization of origin: There is little information about this parasitic and colonizing race, in conjunction with the Anunnaki Race are responsible for the human devolution, by manipulation and stunted spiritual development between constant and uninterrupted wars and resets in most of their colonies. It is believed that they took over 90% of them in former times and used the same for their great technological advancement when most other races were not even developed for their defense.

Their present: It is believed that these beings are in an incessant search to be able to penetrate the great dividing walls or Great Dome, and looking for the connection with the "Celestial Lands" or "Terra-Incognita" and they still continue in their study achieving, as far as we know, great advances to be able to understand what could be found outside the Great Dome and inside the "Terra-Incognita" There is much information about the subway bases and BSM (Mobile Submarine Bases) existing both in their own lands and in the Known Lands, and we also have information about the same type of bases in other lands, but these are very complex to analyze as they change over time their position radically, although at one time followed a certain pattern, after the Great War and the new reset carried out have made major changes throughout its structure.

In our books we find few stories in direct reference to their lands and only one of them seems to have enough strength to be mentioned, it should be clarified that this contact was not direct by any ancestor but through a Giant-Human that approached their lands surrounding them as close as possible before being detected and that I will detail later in this report.

These beings are known for presenting themselves to the natives of different "Surrounding-Circles" with a humanoid figure and upper limb or face shaped like different animal forms that are usually characteristic of each region, and so they were represented in our lands in many of the drawings found within the official history of ancient civilizations.

Their hierarchy stands out for the classic pyramidal shape that they installed in all the sites they colonized and ruled for long periods, its dome is divided in turn into three distinct positions, although these three parts are known as "Leaders" the truth is that only the "Royal-Leaders" are always those who have the last word and carry out the most important decision making.

Story H012-304 in Lands X001 from the book titled (Translated from native ancestral language) as: "**No Parasitic King Will Be Accepted by The Ancestral People**" - Great Capital Ancestral Library - The Ark.

"Mik-ha dared to carry it out, we do not know why, but he broke formation with his ship and was lost in the horizon, although he had told me about his mission by an internal voice that demanded it, the truth is that I never thought he would actually carry it out. I thought it was just a joke or a play on words, but today I saw him for the last time and this would be the last memory of that old friend". Mik-ha was a Giant-Human survivor of the Great War, after settling in the "Ancient Lands of Anak" he sailed with 6 other members of the special forces over the lands they called "Neo-Biz" at that time, they were lands that were used in the beginning as depots and military bases. The Giant-Humans were grouped together as most of the ancestral humanity (that survived the last reset - Sixth Generation) had grouped on other nearby islands, all of them important members of the famous "Great Tartary" the empire that was defeated by the Custodians during the Great War.

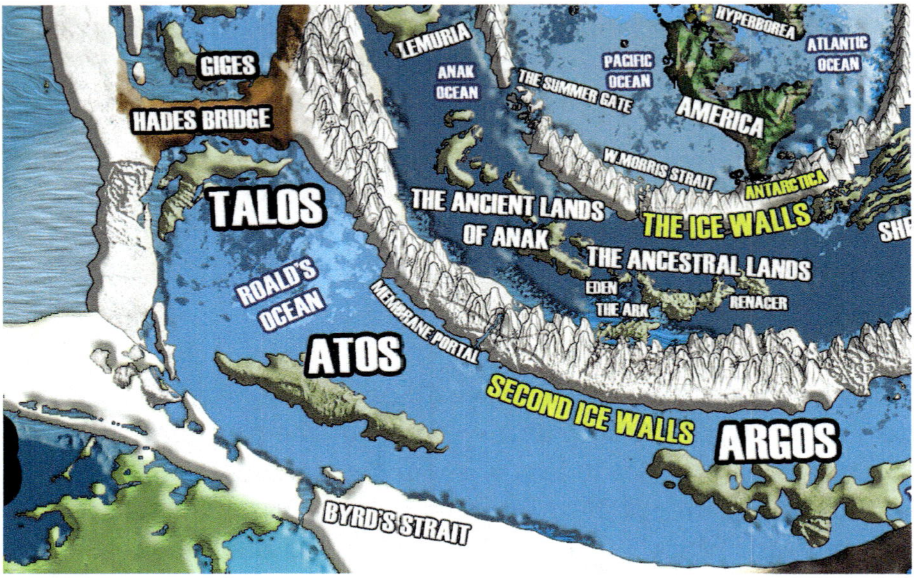

Mik-ha had already commented in several opportunities that to know the enemy it was necessary to approach their lands, by information obtained from some of their bases and reports in bases of the "Greys" in the Known Lands (generally temporary bases during their leadership that would quickly fail before the advance of the Great Tartary) it was known approximately their location in the maps that the "Anakim" Giants had at that time, although the leaders had flatly forbidden him to attempt any approach flight to any region other than the surrounding region between the lands they had taken behind First Dome, Mik-ha seemed to disregard several of these requests, and had flown over the land of "Lemuria" even reaching the lands known as "Laurentia" on several occasions.

The leaders of the special forces were not like military leaders that we usually know in any army of the new humanity, they were quite permissible but clearly advised that any false move could result not only in certain death but would clearly endanger the entire region, they should stay hidden as much as possible and for the longest period of time until, at least, recover their civilization and organize themselves in every possible way.

Mik-ha reached the Second Walls very close to the "Second Dome" and flew over the area to establish some point of union, he was looking for an exit point, a "matter connector" or "Membrane Portal" and he would achieve his goal in one of his many trips following some frozen islands of the Ancient Lands of Anak also close to "The Ark" of the Ancestral Lands.

He studied the area, made calculations and was also helped by several Giants whom he mentioned above and never left names explicitly so as not to blame them for what he was about to do, Mik-ha set off "South" breaking formation and in a determined way directly towards the "Membrane Portal".

Completely breaking the pattern followed by those of his own strength and civilization at the time, there were few records of the Giants outside of the Second Dome, he achieved the unthinkable, and communicated directly with his leader informing him of his new adventure into the unknown lands, "The Custodian Lands".

The Giant leaders met and being aware of the situation, they tried to persuade the young adventurer but everything was rejected and Mik-ha would continue his course flying over "Athos" all over the "Ocean of Roald" something unthinkable for then with an ancestral ship via air. Surrounding the enormous existing walls between the "Lands of Mars" and "Land of Angels", he went through a thick fog and an incredibly high risk bordering the "Lands of Jupiter", this heroic and lonely journey was almost a suicide for the great leaders who already resigned helped Mik-ha's flight to reach its destination, although it was quite uncertain.

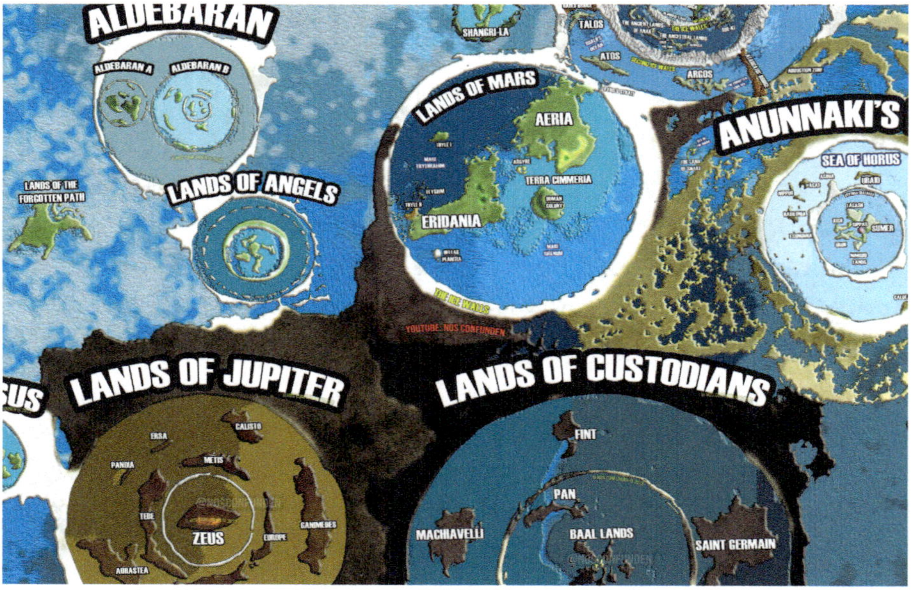

Mik-ha communicated with base trying to explain the little he could visualize, there was a kind of dark wall, totally dark, in fact he had almost hit it among the fog still existing around him, although less thick than before. Those dark walls were the strangest he had ever seen, and some huge towers seemed to emerge from the other side, they were undoubtedly the fearsome Custodian Lands, those enemy lands were in front of him.

The last communication with base was that a red light seemed to be behind him and following his path, it was ruled out that it was an enemy missile by the detail of the pursuit movement, but those would be the last minutes of direct contact with Mik-ha who never communicated again with base nor returned to our lands. His companions tried to persuade the leaders to send ships to his rescue, after three Suns passed, two rescue teams were sent, but they had great inconveniences to overcome the surrounding walls between "Mars" and "Known Lands" and unfortunately they gave missing the young Mik-ha, obtaining great information about the position of the enemy lands, and other surrounding lands since he managed to send details of his scanning achieved from his ship.

LANDS OF CUSTODIANS
FINT
PAN
MACHIAVELLI
BAAL LANDS
SAINT GERMAIN
HERMANDAD
NAGAS
FRATERNITY
HESPERUS
RESURRECTION LANDS
INFERNO

LANDS OF LEMURIA, THE CONNECTION WITH THE BEGINNING OF HUMANITY

Many books can lead to the confusion that the lands of "Lemuria" would be close to "Asgard" because it goes back to the very human creation, or rather, since "The Source" took physical bodies to undertake an arduous and winding path facing those who would later be its parasitic colonizers. For this reason we can find maps of Lemuria close to the famous Atlantis "north" of "Asgard", where it all began. But with the passage of time we have confirmed and updated in our database that Lemuria, which so many references are found even today within the "Walled Lands", is connected to the lands just "north" of "The Ancient Lands of Anak".

These lands were visited on several occasions by the Ancestors, Anakim Giants and Giant-Humans of old Tartary and has a great direct connection to Asgard and the structures that could still be found there, unfortunately reaching the gates of Asgard is far from simple and the Ancestors have suffered many casualties trying to do so, as have other races. It is a very controlled site as it could answer great questions of the existence and history of mankind, as well as we know that there are portals inside and outside our homelands that could connect and transfer matter directly there, although it is very unsafe due to the instability of these.

After the desperation of the inhabitants of Tartary in their escape out of the "First Dome" entire families had to find refuge wherever they could, although the closest lands with which they collided were those mentioned above as "Ancestral Lands", "The Lands of She-Ki" and "The Ancient Lands of Anak" and the same welcomed families escaping from the Great War between humans, giant-humans of Tartary against the Custodians and Anunnaki, also other groups decided to move further away believing that the enemies would still pursue them arriving to the lands behind the First Dome.

For that reason some came to the shores of a new land that was to be "Lemuria" and settled there. The mystery arose when records of strange subway bases of unknown origin were found by means of hatches closed from the inside that prohibited the ancestral humans to go inside and investigate thoroughly. Then with the passage of time five more hatches were discovered along the coast of these new lands, and by means of a message to the leaders, the Anakim Giants approached Lemuria in order to unveil the mystery of the hatches.

It took a long time to penetrate them and then advanced and very strange machinery systems were found there, for this reason the Giants, Giant-Humans and experienced Ancestors joined together to carry out a deep investigation. Although the origin of these structures could never be revealed, it was conjectured that they could belong to a totally advanced hybrid race, since inside there were carried out studies of the manipulation of the temporal and genetic line, remote vision by advanced systems inside matter, and other studies that we cannot expose in these texts, but the study of these lands took another interest on the part of the leaders since the direct connection with Asgard and the beginning of the humanity refloated there.

Today they are inhabited by a strange race that has arrived from outside the Dome, which peacefully integrated into the nearby Ancestral and Anak lands.

THE ARCANE ISLANDS

Ancestral Book - "The Conquering Crowns and Civilizations of Distant Lands" X95-CII / "Humanity Generation II - The Battle of Mount Unai and The Ancient Titans" Book of the Great Ancestral Library in the Capital "The Ark"

In a remote place where few have dared to travel there are lands of great victors who have helped humanity Gen II (Second Generation), their bodies define and make the difference, but more their bravery and dedication to the fight against the conquering parasite. More than a hundred ships landed on the slopes that connect with the dividing Second Ice Wall, from there descended 53 creatures unknown to us at that time, our guard to see such a descent of creatures of more than four meters high that moved in a frantic and fast way, sent their signal Stop! So that they could appear according to engage in a peaceful communication.

The men stopped their descent abruptly and one of them with his hands in the air descended alone towards our position. He introduced himself as "Hulex" and commented that he came from the "Arcane Islands" and that the distance they had traveled was so great that the time-space shift between Domes was playing havoc with their genetics. They asked us for help, among other things, which we were able to exchange, it was a moment to take advantage of since we were just settling in to the new life in the Ancestral Lands, as good hosts we attended them and made their stay the best possible experience.

They thanked us for our hospitality and gave us several plans, technology and also helped with the creation of some of our structures and connecting highways between cities. They also told us the story of their ancestors and how they helped humanity of the past, also failing in their attempt against the oppressive custodian. That ancient humanity of the second generation, who also knew how to forge a great empire and who has left traces of that uprising, as well as the titanic giants "Arcane" that they themselves tell how they proudly helped in the Ancient Known Lands.

Some of their brethren were trapped in those lands in stone form, by the use of the Custodians against a group of humanity that had rebelled. Some of the arcane leaders with their more than four meters high were buried or mimetized in the environment that even today the new humans tread, they rest with their faces surprised by that unknown technology for those times, who stood up for the human liberation like so many other beings of the most recondite surroundings, who know very well that the human deserves full freedom and that the parasites must disappear once and for all from these great and mysterious worlds inside the Great Dome.

ARB013 - ANUNNAKI

Inhabitants: No Information

What we know about their civilization of origin: The originators developed early and sought to expand their knowledge and territory. They are Beings that seek to increase their power by colonizing other lands and other civilizations.

They are known for the creation of pyramidal structures that they use to reset/restart a Circle-Environment, as well as use it for other purposes in the same manipulation/control. They are also known as great creators and manipulators of Portals that transfer matter between distant places. Their development in weapons led them to be able to place themselves next to the Custodians in the dome of absolute power, they are hostile and devoid of any kind of emotion or feeling.

Their present: They are studying the edges of the Great Dome trying, as far as we know unsuccessfully, to be able to cross them. They have large colonies scattered throughout the plane.

There are a large number of Anunnaki leaders scattered throughout the colonized lands, believed to outnumber the

Custodians and to be the most numerous beings within the Great Dome.

There is a great deal of information about their colonization of other lands, some of their technology, and structure of their lands, but penetration into "Erythra Thatassa", the great core of their lands, has never been possible by the Ancestors nor by the Giant-Humans.

The "Abduction Zone" near the "Atargatis Bridge" is a region that the giant leaders, ancestors and giant-humans try to avoid at all costs, it is a forbidden zone and marked in red on the great maps existing even today. The area besides being dangerous and completely hostile, there are also portals many of them in disuse that further complicate any matter that may be nearby, in addition to the existing radars and that some races live or patrol the area in search of other beings lost or transported by ancient portals across the width and length of the "Planets" within the Great Dome.

There is a danger that the Anunnaki may try in conjunction with other races to invade the "Atargatis Bridge" and try to colonize our lands in that position, for that reason, forces were deployed in time to install bases, some of them mobile to try not to be detected, the Anakim Giants deployed and developed technology to anticipate any attack that could come from "Argos" behind the Second Ice Walls.

ANUNNAKI'S LANDS
SEA OF THE MANA
THE LAND OF SNAKE
SEA OF HORUS
ASIRIA
ACAD
UBAID
NIPPUR
ERYTHRA THATASSA
LAGASH
BABILONIA
KISH
SIPPAR
SUMER
ESHNUNNA
URUK
NIMROD LANDS
CALDEA

CONTINUATION OF MORRIS AND BUTLER'S JOURNEY TO THE KNOWN LANDS

CHAPTER 24 - THE INVISIBLE STRUGGLE, THE INNER STRUGGLE

Who would get up and argue today about the stars that are seen in the heavens every night? Or about the Moon or the Sun? Or about everything that is established?

Perhaps very few, it is that the conditioning of a lifetime or, rather, of past lives and lifetimes influences our thinking today, because the vast majority have simply accepted things as they were handed down from childhood.

We will be marginalized in the future if we simply comment this to someone else, we will be taken as insane people who have to be under observation of some professional, that professional who accepted all this, accepted the books he had to recite, accepted the "Earth" that he has walked and lived since he was born, accepted that he had to repeat certain words at the right time so that with a piece of paper and several signatures, he is granted permission to speak or study on certain issues. Who then will discuss about the educational systems? Or about what things should or should not teach us?

The world is empty for being justly full of confused and many times absurd ideas that we were simply adopting as time went by, and without even asking ourselves, we continue with the same plan, the same routine daily, when sometimes in that emptiness an inner voice resounds very loud saying "Hey, something is not right here" in that instant is when we seek to turn off our mind with another kind of thoughts, maybe and most probably some problem that is going around us.

The new generation is becoming and adapting every day more and more in simple robotic actions, it is far away from the previous one and it is already a mere spectrum of its first version, its competition with the other and its life based on mere biological functions is self-destructive, besides being easily manipulated, for this and many other reasons going into those lands where I was born become very difficult, because not only we fight against parasites but against many people who were contaminated by this manipulation under the same parasitic reign.

It is the price paid by humanity as a whole to fight for a freedom that never came, until now, and it remains to be discovered if we will be able to achieve it. It seems difficult being in these lands so polluted but even more being from outside, those lands are ours, they belong to us, as well as our absolute freedom and our infinite spiritual growth, human life was born with a purpose, "The Source" of the Celestial Lands took physical bodies to take care of this Great Dome, the races that inhabit it, and of course, to return the parasitic colonizers to their original form, the use of technology to dominate and crush into dictatorial control another entire race and not only prevent them from leaving but also manipulate their bodies, minds, their surroundings and their future is simply macabre and can only be carried out by utterly despicable beings.

I do not like to generate division even when it comes to these beings, but they have made of this Great Dome that offers the most beautiful beings, sights and places anyone has ever seen, a hellish place with constant fights, manipulation, control, psychological games and only for personal gain and search to increase their own power, but everything has an end and this is the gateway that will take us beyond, our growth and knowledge of our past and surrounding lands have to come to light, although as I said before, this places us in a place as dark as the distant seas crossing the Great Dome, the marginality is latent for those of us who dare to even ask that question that many hate due to the comfort they acquired, can we live otherwise?

Can we even call this freedom? Being in my homeland, there is a lot of noise and mental interference that originates especially in the big cities, the tumult, the rush and the absolute disorganization make the whole experience something difficult to digest.

People here run without really knowing why, are in a hurry to live, and focus or should I say "focus" one on the importance of physical appearance and the volatile achievements they carry in the mere environment What would happen then if one lives simply without having an image of oneself?

We should try to find out what would happen then with all that mental interference if our image disappears from one day to the next, I mean what you think of yourself, of the achievements and failures, of all the problems that your own mind has created for you, maybe the awakening is closer than we think simply with small changes. In the world around you right now you will never find the answer that we are immense because our spiritual growth is so, we are the purest creation that the parasites do not want to release, we are their greatest opposition that exists in this Great Dome for the dirtiest parasites of all, if only you could discover it for yourself in the silence, when your thoughts are silent and there is stillness, when you can see your surroundings in another way, without so much interference, without so much manipulation, you are not a coincidence or a mere point in the false universe, you are so important that they should have imprisoned you under Walls and manipulated your body, your environment, your history for seven long generations, the path to "awakening" is not to be better than another, it is not about that, it is about a path that sooner or later we will all walk, it is simply to realize how great it is to live this moment, despite being under the domination of these corrupt beings, a chain that we can break, not to let this state of unhappiness that in general seems to lead the new humanity be something accepted without questioning it at all.

Among so many thoughts Butler sat down again next to me, the great Captain, who had so many stories that made of himself a living encyclopedia, he had sailed so many seas that many of his stories could also be found in the Great Ancestral Library, not in vain I brought some of these books, to continue assembling this great puzzle, Butler knew very well how to enter and exit through the First Dome, he had done it several times until, at least, the discovery of the Custodians about the Portal we had opened and the military fortification with the installation of the thousands of bases that had been operating there for some time, and above all, because of the system of earthquake generating radars in the area.

Things had become complicated to sneak inside, but we were willing to do it once again even with the pain I felt throughout my body was nothing compared to the possibility of returning to the land where I was born and see my brothers again.

CHAPTER 25 - THE HIDDEN LAND NEAR ANTARCTICA

How would we do it this time? Well, by air, Butler would sentence, and it would be the first time for me to penetrate the First Dome with the famous "Iron Blue." This had to have surgical precision and was very risky, but considering the security moves that were taking place around the Ice Walls, it was better to be safe and do it by air.

That same afternoon we left for the Old Continents, I felt as much adrenaline as excitement inside me, I could not wait to take off, our great ship departed ascending at an incredible speed and reaching a height that I had never reached in my previous trips, you could clearly see the waters above over the Second Dome, everything was calm and according to plan, at least, until we approached the dividing edge.

It was planned to pass through the passage we were already well acquainted with Butler since my boat had long before sailed across, but this time, with a ship crossing the skies and going at great speed. Butler, knowing me, remarked several times to put my mind at ease, that everything would go as planned, there were only four of us inside, the pilot and one person who could indicate by sound alone what was the fault of those bluish beasts that were cruising the skies.

We descended several feet to reach an altitude that we considered, a priori, "safe" since the radars should not detect us, suddenly we entered this passage and the experience by air is totally different, it is to enter a kind of tunnel where nothing is heard but silence, the speed although we had reduced it considerably before entering, there inside it seemed that we were being shaken frantically, everything lasted seconds and we appeared on the other side, flying upside down over the Antarctic sea.

The pilot quickly and with great astuteness controlled the ship and the situation brilliantly, everything returned to normal as the ship righted its course. The Ice Walls were perfectly visible, we were at about 2300 feet altitude.

We crossed part of the Walls without problems, but something was not right with our ship, several alarms went off inside and we began to lose altitude rapidly, we saw land in sight on the south coast, and the Lanner pilot made an emergency landing, everything was starting to go wrong in our return to the Known Lands, was this the unexpected end just minutes after returning to my beloved lands?

The Iron Blue broke into the quiet wooded areas between huge snowy mountains and with great care we managed to survive a forced but incredible landing between trees that hit our most precious bird that moved us and resisted the onslaught, one after another, we went from one side to the other, until suddenly peace invaded, we had passed the first test, but now what? I asked, Butler was beaten, but he was fine, and the other two ancestors had no major injuries either, my leg hurt quite a bit from the blows and my body too, although as you know, I had come with some problems since before entering these lands.

It remained to find out if this abrupt fall had been an error of our ship (something that was quite difficult to imagine) or if it had been caused by some technology that had been installed by the parasites or the forces that worked for them.

We were on some remote islands on the border with the Walls, which could not be seen in the distance due to the fog that covered the great forests but we knew exactly that they were there. The sun was peeking through the large trees and we left quickly to get away from the ship, in case there were forces in the area that could have spotted our fall.

We were mere mortals coming from the other side of the Walls, with a broken ship, strange clothing, although similar to the time that ran in my homeland, with ancient technology that fortunately still worked properly, but really if they wanted to attack us was our worst time and the worst way to have entered. We moved away about 900 meters from the area of the fall, although it had been resounding our ship had not generated any fire or something to consider that we could have been spotted from afar, the fog invaded completely and we could barely make out the road we were traveling in these cold forests.

Suddenly we began to hear strange noises coming from the north, someone was walking in the weeds, the fog prevented us from seeing if it was a man and we decided to stop our march completely. We crouched down in the thick grass and waited.

10,20,30 seconds passed and nothing, silence invaded, so one minute, two minutes, it was even five, when we overcame this we came out of the trees and ran head on into a human soldier walking towards us, I think we were both stunned, but the marine touched his gun with his left hand and raised his right to indicate that he would not shoot and immediately called us silently to come closer to his position.

Butler indicated that we should follow him and not say a word, he would speak, then the soldier asked us in perfect English what battalion we were from or where we came from, we let the Captain speak and he gave him concrete answers and exact locations to dispel any doubts from the soldier, we began to have equally great suspicions of this marine, what was he really doing patrolling alone in these latitudes? We were not even aware that humans had reached this remote southern part of the known continents.

Charlie, as the soldier introduced himself, received us in the best way believing Butler's version and handed us several fruits and food that he carried in his backpack, while he began to tell us about how he arrived to these lands and how confused he was in his way.

CHAPTER 26 - THE SOLDIER'S INFORMATION ON THE WAR BETWEEN HUMANS AND GIANTS IN HIDDEN LANDS IN THE SOUTH

Charlie patted my right shoulder and began to give me the "condolences" for being there too, "Human brothers, it is always good to see a brother walking beside me" Charlie commented strangely, we doubted his mental health at that moment, and not because there were not other beings around but we doubted that he was really aware, then we were going to understand the situation and what he meant in a perfect way.

I understand that you are new and surely you haven't seen the "killer beasts" commented Charlie, we all looked at each other without fully understanding, Charlie then continued: "Friends, it will be quite interesting to see your faces when you see those beasts coming against you in a hurry, I will understand since I have seen the same expression in everyone here".

Listen, what "beasts" are you telling us about? Butler asked, rather confused.

- "You'll see them," Charlie said, and then pointed his rifle towards the horizon to the east.

-There, look over there," he continued, "That one lying there, that's one of the beasts, you'll see it move in seconds, hold on."

We all stared at that sector and a Giant suddenly stood up, it would be about five meters tall, it was an incredible being and another race of Giants that I did not know in person.

"The blue beings, did you talk to the blue beings?" Charlie commented Again we made gestures of not understanding.

Charlie then commented:

- "You are the strangest new agents in this area," he then sentenced, "But time to time, you already saw and had the first experience with one of the beasts, and you will understand everything promptly."

Clearly being able to understand that situation could be beneficial to us, with a ship in shambles, the Custodians who seemed to walk all around us, in the most recondite land and at the mercy of Giants who knew little and nothing about us.

- "This war makes no sense at all," Charlie commented.

- "Rather none of it does, but this one much less so, we are at war against beings we didn't even know existed until now, that they don't understand our culture and only act out of repetition or defense, you know what I mean? It is a repetition, a loop that never stops, over and over again the same thing, every day like being in limbo itself.

- "I thank the Lord you guys showed up, I thought I was going crazy and ... I almost committed insanity, we must get out of here soon" commented Charlie already in a desperate way.

Butler tried to calm him down and sat him on a large rock and gave him water so that he could relax, Charlie's experiences clearly showed that they came from a Machiavellian and perverse game, from what other sector could this come more than the damned parasites? With Butler we understood it perfectly, although we did not yet know the details or in depth about these "beasts" as Charlie called them, we knew clearly that this game was about the Custodians and these lands were somehow hidden to perform this "kind of perverse game" although what was the function of all that?

CHAPTER 27 - THE CUSTODIAN GAME - THE WAR BETWEEN HUMANS AND GIANTS IN HIDDEN LANDS IN THE SOUTH

While Charlie recovered his breath and could calm down a little when he saw beings of his own race around him, we asked him questions to better understand the situation that surrounded us, and that we were going to have to face if we wanted to get out of there alive.

The answers would begin to give us a little light to navigate this new path that destiny had in store for us.

Charlie then began to detail his mysterious move to these hidden lands while an intense rain suddenly fell and meanwhile we were seeking shelter among rocks stained with mud.

"I can't understand how I got to these lands, because the final destination was to reach a base in Antarctica, or so we were told by a military man who claimed to be in charge, we had never seen him before, some of us were sent to a precarious base in southern Argentina, we were put on a warship, they explained the basics about the mission we were supposed to carry out in the Antarctic Peninsula, and it was only about logistics, guiding and taking care of the scientists who were going to transport elements for meteorological studies, that was basically what we were informed, among the military chiefs there were also other people with strange dark clothes, they seemed to come out of another time, they had dark glasses and did not seem to look directly at us, but avoided us or ignored us completely."

"Some companions asked some questions and gave us to drink something they said was obligatory, as I drank that rather disgusting and thick liquid my legs began to feel a strange tingling sensation, then my waist, then my chest seemed to burst, and I fainted. I woke up among the rocks and the swamp, while unknown people were running and screaming in pain around me, I had this gun you see and just as I was, I got up and started shooting at the beasts that were slowly approaching from afar, almost for the same survival, none seemed to understand the situation around, There was only one very quiet man who was sitting looking at the ground, but his calmness was really admirable, I approached him and shouted several times for him to follow us, those beasts were taking soldiers with their hands and were shaking them on the ground as if they were made of paper, the nightmare was beginning".

- Butler: Have you come across any of those strange beings with dark glasses around here? Or those blue beings? Who are those beings?

- Charlie: "The Blue Beings appeared before us when we spent the sixth night here, we moved away from the focus where those beasts seem to live, and secluded ourselves along the coast, we tried not to light fires, but the cold and hunger become a worse struggle than those beasts when they go whole days without tasting any food, then we had no choice but to make small and divided during the daylight so as not to raise so much suspicion, or so we imagined. But as I was telling you, after the sixth night, very early in the morning when the sun was just rising, a large boat appeared on the horizon and approached until it got as close to the coast where we were, three of those blue beings appeared overboard, they were very strange because the sun hit behind them and seemed to go through them. The sunlight turned blue when it "touched" their bodies, many of our companions who were camping there tried to swim towards the boat as an escape route, I do not blame them since I also thought so, but from the boat they started to shoot at them, confusion reigned among us again, we had huge beasts behind the vegetation waiting for us, and from the sea a boat arrived to shoot at us, how could we explain this whole experience?

This boat after killing several soldiers moved away throwing several huge boxes near the shore, we did not trust them at all after the most chilling scene we could live, but we thought that maybe it was information, something that would explain or give us a certain path to follow, or at least some food, so we had no choice but to bring them and open them as soon as possible. Inside them were more weapons of war, more advanced weapons than we had so far, grenades, and some night vision binoculars, in one of the three large boxes were sheets that in addition to detailing the inventory that had been sent to us, who knows what for or why, also had the list of all our names, and underneath it said something like:

"Freedom is obtained by killing the Seven Giants that live in these islands, once the last one is dead, the exit will be automatically enabled"

Some groups took weapons and left to the West side, others went to another sector, and some others stayed there trying to process everything, it was a very complex situation, and the division of the members was going to be even worse, at least I sensed it.

The following nights were even more terrible, we could hear gunshots, explosions and all kinds of screams of pain in the distance, one of those nights we saw how a soldier was shot through the air and the deafening scream of the beasts was chilling.

There were only eight of us left in our group, we decided to stay together no matter what, we approached one of the beasts without knowing it and it began to chase us emitting piercing sounds.

I am not sure how long we ran in the opposite direction to retreat, time in these lands is very strange to analyze, but this being reached us and when it was less than two meters from us it grabbed one of us with both hands, I shot him several times while running without thinking, one of the shots happened to enter through his right eye and the giant with a scream of excruciating pain fell down on top of the soldier who had between his hands. We seized the moment to run with all our might, lamenting another casualty and this time a very close one, I had known him for a long time, almost since I joined the army, he was like a brother to me.

Butler then interrupted saying that we were very sorry for his loss and that he had to go on with strength as we were clearly in danger, this absurd war against the Giants was a perverse game of the parasites, we don't quite know what the purpose would be, but many times it is impossible to come to a conclusion of the sick games they make the new humans play and especially with other races, especially the race they detest like the Giants.

Anyway, Butler knew that these Giants had no relation to the ones we knew, and they seemed to be genetically modified in an obvious way, they were possibly imprisoned here on these islands and might even have been moved from the Antarctic land itself to here to carry out this kind of manipulation.

Two of the giants suddenly appeared behind the rocks where we were waiting, one in front and one behind our position, they had us cornered, Charlie shouted something like "I am exhausted of this reality, damned giants" and ran towards one of them shooting with his rifle, the Giant was receiving bullet impacts but in the first seconds it seemed not to do him any damage, He had in his right hand a big piece of metal that he took to the top to take impulse and let fall from his fist with all the force to where Charlie was, who lost his life in the act, the Giant fell down defeated by the previous shots and we had no other option but to escape, we were terrified and confused.

The Giant that appeared on the opposite side did not follow us, we believe that when he saw his comrade killed he decided to retreat, we returned for Charlie's body to deposit it on the nearby coast.

Although it seemed a parallel reality, there was then hidden lands where a perverse war manipulated by the Custodians was taking place, where humans and a race of Giants were facing each other, the rules and weapons were given by the colonizing parasites to enjoy the bloody and brutal confrontations, how long had this been going on? I wondered.

Charlie had died like so many other soldiers, who were delivered as offerings to giant beings genetically modified and also used for this confrontation, we traveled another part of the coast and found no more survivors, this situation was another of the many that we had to stop, exterminate it at the root, clearly the parasites ruled, they felt they were the owners and were willing to take this manipulation to all levels.

Butler did not understand how this area was not known after so many previous trips and how we were not aware of it, but we could not focus on that at this time, although it should be clarified that Butler felt something different about the "reality" we were living there, anyway, we had to start planning our escape from those cursed islands near Antarctica. We couldn't leave our ship broken down in the middle of that forest either, for if they were found they would know perfectly well that the ancestors had returned to their homelands, if they weren't already aware of it by then.

Butler commented in passing that possibly the Custodians were using the race of Giants they called "Patagons" by moving them here, undergoing serious genetic modification and all that it entailed just to satisfy their pleasure of another cruel war. As he was saying that out loud as a form of catharsis and explaining in passing his idea about these lands, we were approaching a metallic gray structure and the beings standing at its gates were not going to be friendly to us at all but quite the opposite, Custodians, men in black and military men of the new humanity were there in some sort of meeting that seemed to be of the high command, as Butler would later confirm the presence of a Custodian Leader, according to our records he was known as

"Agares" and there he was entering through a space inside this strange grayish colored structure right under our noses.

What do we do now? I asked aloud, confused by the whole situation and it was not for less, we were really in a critical moment, Butler nodded his head and knew then that we should return to our ship, I guessed then that he planned to send a rescue signal, but it was too high risk, in fact, I did not even think we would use that option ever. The truth is that we were really at a dead end since we didn't know this island, the ship couldn't stay there and we had a whole Custodian meeting going on in front of us.

We hurried as much as we could in our return to the forest, the signal would be sent immediately and it could cause us to be detected by the radars, not only in the air but also on the ground, and those would generate an earthquake of high levels around us, the Custodians would come out in search of us and the worst end would await us, what would happen then? Was it time to take a risk and look for a way out? Although I must also clarify that looking for a way out of that strange area was not very encouraging either.

CHAPTER 28 - THE RESCUE

Butler and our pilot Lanner had a heated talk where they could not agree, but inside the ship Lanner commented that we had a system to track and/or communicate with any other Ancestor that was piloting or even navigating in the vicinity, it served only with short distance frequencies, he called it the "OP.05" it was also risky to activate it but by then where there were discrepancies and also activating the other plan was even more dangerous, Lanner carried out the rescue plan of sending a signal to try to look for help in the surroundings.

We understood that we were close to the Antarctic Peninsula and there could be camouflaged ancestors in one of the bases operating there, the signal was sent and we waited a few minutes, Butler took the time we could not exceed 5 minutes 50 seconds, and so it was then that they were passing .... the first, nothing, the second, nothing, the third, nothing and the fourth was answered, in an incredible way and as a divine message we had located ancestors near the area (or so we thought) they headed towards us but during the wait the murmurs began again, we could not really know for sure that those who were coming for us were really ancestors or were sent by the parasites that had taken our technology, the next twenty minutes were in complete silence and we prepared ourselves as we could for a possible confrontation.

A small but modern boat arrived at the shores of that strange island, from there two people headed towards our meeting with an inflatable boat of those used for offshore rescue or simply to save themselves when the boat is in the last hours afloat.

Two agents introduced themselves as Josh and Riant, Butler greeted them cordially and Lanner fortunately knew them both, I think from both parties we breathed a deep sigh of relief as they later commented that they were also approaching thinking that perhaps it was a Custodian trap that had somehow picked up our signal using an OP.05.

Josh and Riant commented that they were very disturbed on the Peninsula and all bases alerted to earthquakes (hence many Ancestors were being detected). They also told in a very technical way to our pilot Lanner that the technology used there had changed dramatically in recent times and surely that was the reason that had made our ship in inoperable condition while in flight, so they believed that many brothers had fallen without much chance of survival, even if they could be ejected, the ocean at those latitudes was like falling into millions of needles sticking in the body at the same time, hypothermia would not take long to do its thing, in this way the Custodians knocked down any possibility of infiltration but the ships would not always be detected.

Josh and Riant were doing intelligence service being able to infiltrate human military bases with direct connection to some informant-mediator who spoke directly to high Custodian commanders, they generally used these islands, the most recent and what they were really upset about was possible infiltration in the Known Lands by Giants, that was even worse for them, since they clearly knew that in the not so distant past they could take away the custody of their most precious colony, the humanity of these walled lands.

Josh commented that She-Ki was possibly the one who had infiltrated these lands, Butler as I have rarely seen his eyes widened, he was blown away by that information, "She-Ki, you say? SHE-KI?" Lanner was also surprised asking almost the same question. Josh let a smile show nervously and Riant clarified that they were possibly looking for the connector portal number 609, that's when Butler and Lanner looked at each other even more confused than before, for what reason, what was the plan, what were the Giants looking for in that connection? I was once again, almost separated from them trying to remember the thousands of books I had read over and over again in the Ancestral database, I did not remember the numbers of the portals, in fact, there was not so much information on this subject, and the one there was did not reference those numbers, then I tried again to be part of this conversation and took advantage of the situation of complete confusion between Lanner and Butler, then I asked:

- What portal? What is Portal 609?

The one that leads to the gates of Asgard, said almost at the same time Josh and Riant. So now I joined the confusion and the same faces of Lanner and Butler, we really did not understand why She-Ki and the Giant-Humans sought to enter Asgard, also risking everything.

While Captain Josh's small boat took us all out of a very

dangerous area as those southern islands between the Peninsula and the coasts of South America, we headed to areas a little safer, it should be noted that the ship had been completely destroyed with an ancestral system to carry out in situations like ours, we could not leave any trace that we had visited these lands and less a few steps away from a Custodian leader.

There were conversations about the plan that cannot be included here, but it was about the various human generations and the connection with the Anakim giants and other races as well. The gates of Asgard in the first generations were guarded by species of colossal sizes as it appears in several books of the ancient histories of the new humanity, for example, in Norse mythology and the serpent called "Jörmundgander". The Custodians had then brought several of these giant species from other worlds to guard the gates of Asgard and surroundings, why so much mystery there? Well, it was first necessary to understand that in these lands humanity was forged, the human bodies were taken by "The Source" from the "Celestial Lands", it is the place where it all began.

The direct connection that existed with Hyperborea, or "the core of the Known Lands" was destroyed, but Portal 609 was known by then to be still operational, without being able to give any great information about it either, it was between great mountains between what is known as Europe and Asia. Everything then began to close in my mind, first the great confusion of learning that the great and beautiful She-Ki who had given me her book and all the information that revealed in me and in all my group at that time a reality that I did not know completely, and thus gave me the necessary strength to return and try together with the ancestors to free my brothers that I had left behind and what I thought I would never see again.

Now then I could imagine that She-Ki knew of our journey and our plan to these lands, and his journey to the gates of Asgard was intrinsically related, Was She-Ki helping us to carry out this plan of human liberation? It was a possibility, a great possibility!

CHAPTER 29 - SHE-KI AND THE HUMAN-GIANTS SEEK THE DOORS TO ASGARD

In our excitement of interesting and deep conversations about everything that was happening there, we forgot for a moment that we were somehow escaping from the lands of the leader Agares. While it was true that they seemed unaware of our unplanned visit, the fact was that their technology had caused our ship to fall to earth like two magnets, a signal had been sent to the "Antarctic Peninsula" and two agents had arrived in a boat to their shores, it was highly unlikely that any of them had noticed our visit, but by then I think, we preferred to imagine that nothing could go wrong by then.

Josh had given us the information of where the infiltrated ancestors were located in several nearby points, most of them in military bases there, in this way we wrote down every corner to be able to visit them, we needed one of them to somehow provide us with a ship to return us to our lands, it was clear by then that the main mission we were about to carry out was not going to be possible due to the distance we were in, and with all the traces we could have left, it would be more than risky to carry it out with a secondary ship, we would not only put at risk our lives, but also the lives of every ancestral individual that would help us along the way, and also all the inhabitants of the lands behind the Ice Walls, the Ancestral Lands.

Clearly one of my desires now was to know what was happening with She-Ki and her plan towards Asgard, I regretted not being able to get there to see it, would the structures of the first humans still be there? The first great humans who settled and where it all began, to later fight in the first fateful clash against the parasites.

We sailed between small channels through the south of the continent, and we arrived to what Josh would tell us would be our final destination, since they had to return immediately and from there we should visit several points indicated by them that could rescue us, my body was really sore and dizzy, the ancestral medicine kept me still standing and with some strength, but I think more strength was provided by the fact that I would be able to make contact again with the society of the new humanity, my brothers that I had left so long ago.

CHAPTER 30 - THE CUSTODIAN'S TRAP IN THE SOUTH

Butler, as I always said, was the most experienced and possessed of an "innate nose" for all this sneaking around and not being found, I by then was between the pain in my body and my excitement to step on these lands again and see the faces of the families there walking around us, then the captain said to me:

"William, we must hurry to find these people, clearly something is not right here" It was not common for Butler to say these words unless there was real danger, no doubt he feared for our lives, my excitement was short lived and a deep crisis would echo inside me.

We visited several nearby points, but we did not find the agents and each visit was more and more risky, we were exposing ourselves enough that some military man would become suspicious and might report it to his superiors, and I think we already know what some superiors might do next.

When we had about four more points left, we visited an old hangar near a port, all gray and black numbers on the outside, Lanner spoke at each visit with his strange Spanish accent, one person called another, and another called another, and suddenly five people were surrounding us and asking us questions, I did not understand well what they meant but seeing Lanner's face and their posture was not pleasant.

I suppose they thought we were spies or envoys from another part of the continent or lands, indeed, we were in some way, but not as they surely imagined. One of the agents we were supposed to meet was present on the scene, and for some reason, which again I put down to divinity, the waters calmed down among the military, and with only this agent left with us, we gave him some information Josh had given us so he would know of our urgency and need.

The agent confirmed that he had a ship for us but not here, and we had to make a 318 kilometer trip to the north, he would come with us and so we could then enter the base where that jealously guarded and guarded by the ancestral infiltrated agents. We were not going to wait much longer, everything was getting quite strange around us, we felt people following us everywhere we went, Butler was quite tense, perhaps as he had never noticed before, and the next morning we left for the military base in the north.

The trip was short and we made it via land, when we arrived at this field where there was nothing but trees and overgrown grass that made it difficult for us to walk, another hangar appeared before us, but smaller than the previous one.

We crossed some military points where the agent spoke for us, and we passed one by one. I had little feeling in my legs, the pain was intense and it was hard to walk, in fact at the end Lanner had to help me to get into a kind of very old "elevator", the structure was in a very bad condition due to the notorious disuse and passage of time.

This improvised elevator took us several meters underground, every meter we descended the nauseating smell mixed with humidity intensified. To our surprise, there were two ships there, one was similar to the one that had fallen and the other smaller, spotless, although full of dust, there was a majestic track to be able to go outside and get lost in the skies of the Known Lands, I breathed deeply again, although there was little oxygen down there, I looked at Butler who was still worried, and that was clearly a bad sign.

Butler commented to prepare the two ships and almost "forced" the agent to accompany us, he commented that he would help him in the flight since he was not so used to fly those, the agent commented that he could only help him with the small ship, and then Lanner agreed with Butler so that I would travel with our pilot, Butler would go in the small one next to the agent.

The agent informed us the path we were to follow and incorporated it into the destination of the ship, Lanner began pre-flight duties, checking every point in conjunction with the agent, then the four of us would do it in the small ship, the agent also informed us what we were to do when we arrived at the Ancestral Lands in case for some reason he did not arrive (this was commonplace in travel between worlds passages but nevertheless one prefers to avoid hearing it), who we were to talk to and that the ship be replenished immediately as it was needed for the times to come. I believed then that everyone was preparing for something big, very big, it was not my imagination that the plan was being carried out, and beyond the mistakes made, there was a great light of hope, all this was possible.

We got on the ships, the agent gave orders to two people there who opened some doors that led to a dark tunnel that we had to cross and then go outside, so was our departure from the beautiful lands of the south, lands of my brothers of the new humanity and those forgotten giants, it was certainly a "See you later" as I knew the area better and I had thought in my mind that the next ancestral visits could release much of humanity by air, at least I was excited about that.

CHAPTER 31 - FROM BUTLER'S EYES

The flight plan was correct, the speed and altitude were the right ones, everything was green light inside, but the alarms would soon turn on, and two ships began to follow us as we crossed the well known "Drake Passage".

The great concern now was clearly to be able to leave behind these ships that were chasing us, once confirmed that they were custodian maneuvers were initiated to move away from them, but everything was in vain, I was in permanent contact with Lanner from my ship, our great and experienced pilot assured that these ships could never cross the First Dome, I asked him several times to confirm, Lanner was even approaching the ships in a very risky way to reach a final determination, and the verdict was sentenced, never those custodian ships piloted surely by military of the new humanity could cross the First Dome, how the Custodians could deliver technology of this type to a confused humanity? It was a sign of total desperation not to lose their colony.

As Lanner stated, our ships were heading straight for the Ice Walls and over the plateau we increased speed to maximum. Again, precision would be essential, the Dome was meters away, I looked at Lanner's big ship and he gave me the order to get behind it so I could enter the passage following it. The two pursuing ships knowing the situation moved away from us, as our great pilot had stated, one turned to the right and another would turn to the left, the great concern was dissipating and it was time to cross the First Dome.

Lanner was ahead and I always had my point fixed on him, from one second to another as these tragedies happen in flight and at a similar speed, Lanner's ship crashed in front of us, I did not even have time to process it, my partner in the middle of absolute desperation and where only a second can annihilate you completely, took control, reduced the speed and put the front of the ship in the direction of the sky, I felt fire in my shoulder and right leg, but the deep pain was nothing of what was happening in my body, but that which I did not want to assimilate, that which I feared since we crossed this same passage when we entered, William Morris had died and took with him a great part of all of us.

Our ship had miraculously overcome that invisible wall imposed by the Custodians since we crossed the passage and they detected our route, the agent that I will call "Antony" so as not to reveal his identity, had been the hero who saved my life, The first thing I tried to do after crossing that passage was to return, but Antony kept repeating over and over again that there was nothing to do, and that they had undoubtedly led us into this ambush.

CHAPTER 32 - A NEW TARTARY

It is complex to interpret and digest a death, be it there within their lands or outside of them, be it in other worlds, wherever it happens, my father will always be present with me here in my heart, and not only in mine, in the hearts of so many ancestors who accept that William Morris was not only a visitor, but the one who led us all to better understand the atrocities that are carried out and suffered by the brothers of the new humanity.

And each one of the modifications that our bodies suffered from birth, whatever the generation, each one was entering a perverse and manipulated world, made our world a worse one every day, they not only contaminate their environment, but also their genetics so that each year is not a fruitful year but one less of life. Humanity is sick and slowly dies because of the famous aging that they call "natural process", they will fill their mouths talking about epigenetic alterations, telomeres, cellular senescence and many other factors to explain something that we believe that many leaders or people at the top know perfectly well, the alteration that human bodies suffer in the Circle-Environment, the environment vitiated by the custodian hands, and those pyramids that observe and define in the distance when to start the cycle.

We do not leave the plan to free humanity aside, it is our main goal, even when we know that we put at risk the lives of everyone behind the Ice Walls and the First Dome, all the lands that surround it and all the nearby civilizations that exist, as we already know She-Ki in her journey to the gates of Asgard could change history, a new path and strategy was opened forever and my father knew it perfectly since he learned of that movement, the Giants-Humans plunged back into the mud and that means that we will accompany them, we cannot let our ancestral brothers die in vain, giants and new humans who fought and fight for their lands, my dear father William Morris knew it and he came back here to tell us about his reunion with the brothers of the new humanity and also to say that She-Ki had returned to the Known Lands and was heading to Asgard, where it all began, and we then, have a mission to carry on just as my father wanted, today also begins here the path to human liberation, the Giants and the ancestral humanity unite for a new beginning, A New Tartary!

REFLECTION BY HELEN MORRIS

CHAPTER 33 - HELEN MORRIS RESPONDS - MANIPULATION OF THE NEW HUMANITY

For the colonizing parasites to turn love into something cold and stereotyped, seems to be without a doubt their great primary mission, to turn it into a mere contract with guidelines to fulfill, it is a path full of pain that is only based on a contractual attachment, that is a purely physical choice and that is also based on pre-established images, added to the fear of the unknown, in the end and social alienation is unquestionable, here the individual is punished and pressured for so many things that it is almost so difficult to imagine that another life is possible.

It is similar to the work life and other aspects of life that you lead here, the system that they have created is so rooted in evil that it is repulsive, they make humans believe that they are this way by nature when the reality is that humanity would absolutely reject any type of war or conflict, only that in their minds is the same hostile system that they themselves implanted to carry it forward and make it develop every day without even being detected.

This system feeds back to you, and the answer is not to run

away from it, but to take it from another perspective, from the same silence, the answer is intrinsically connected to be able to collapse in a single instant all the acquired conditioning, this is easier for children because they are not so contaminated, but the reality is that any human born after the last reset can do it, simply in the silence where you have no image of yourself, nor any image from outside, nor from the past, nor try to identify, it is the purest silence that anyone can find, then from there you can find a different answer than the one you would find with limited thinking, you would only hit against the walls that the same mind creates every day, with infinite negative possibilities that will lead you to pain, suffering and mere anxiety.

Love is pure nature, it is beyond the observer and the observed, beyond experience or desire, it is behind all that, you simply must get away from the chip you carry in your modern human mind, from the millions of messages you are bombarded with every day, from the tragedies you imagine in your mind that may never happen or will happen, you must spontaneously get away from the hatred of the colonizing parasites.

They were the ones who molded the new mind of the human because it would be more difficult for you to find the way, the true history of your own past. I understand that all this may be too much to process, and may be misinterpreted, therefore, we will leave it here for the time being.

CHAPTER 34 - YOUR REALITY IS A SIMULATION

What can we do to free ourselves from the reigning custodian yoke?

There are many ways to achieve abstraction even at the very moment you are being punished, sometimes your life can become a torture, it is another part of the Custodian system, your life will have to be in constant danger and alert, you will seek security, and who do you think will offer you security? Bingo! the Custodians.

The indicated thing is that you can try to turn off those thoughts that at every moment your mind is transmitting to you about how or why you are going to perform some action, that does not mean that you should jump into the abyss, but in the figurative sense, then I could say that you should jump into the spiritual abyss, do you understand me? Crossing the dreaded gap between the reality you create through the custodian system and the hidden reality behind all limited thinking, the reality you are living is simply a lie, something properly simulated, you are in a system and even if you are immensely rich or incredibly lucky, you will feel the same emptiness as a person in a system, you will feel the same emptiness as a person who is in the opposite conditions, because that emptiness is your own memory that is latent but forgotten behind all the negative thoughts of your own mind, that memory is the Ancestral, it is the memory of your true past that is screaming to awaken, it is "The Source" that you know very well but you have been made to forget. Simply because by remembering who you are then you would also remember the true origin of humanity, then the parasitic race would have to force a new reset as it happened before.

What are they doing here?

The confusion is tremendous, they have you by the hands and feet, there is not much you can do (physically I mean), it is not possible a physical fight between you and them, there is no such technology nor any possibility, not even remote that they can be defeated today, nor is there any way to reach an understanding with them, they will never let go of their most precious colony on their own. You will always feel fear walking on a path that has no reference, there is no trail ahead to follow, you are alone on this path, you will feel fear and many other sensations, but like all costly achievements, you will enjoy double in the end, more important will be the reward of understanding who surrounds you at this moment, which lands are beyond, so far it is a mystery that we will solve today, clearly you can choose between this path and the other, the one you have been walking so far, but at least here you can get a forgotten knowledge and with it you will decide if you want to keep it and share it, or let it die forever.

THE HUMAN RESET OF THE FIFTH GENERATION

Ancestral Book - "Fifth Generation, Rescue during the end of the cycle - The Age of Giants 0503-X2".

CHAPTER 35 - THE TERROR COMING FROM THE SKY

02:58AM - I was in my room, somewhat restless and fearful for this new night, what would happen this time? I asked myself over and over again as the "watering time" as we had named this particular phenomenon approached. It would start at 3:00 AM as it had been happening lately, and many of us, excluding my father, were expectantly locked up looking out of the windows, waiting.

There was a generalized fear in the population, even though we had created new accesses to our homes where the water could not filter, as well as through the robust fortifications, and we had decided to leave the "home-scanners", even the old low frequency radars that some considered "conspiranoids" said they could detect the causes of this "Irrigation" out there in the dark in many specific points, and even inside our crops.

Darkness was said to be the best way to scare the "Waterers" away, but, the concern had become a worldwide thing, we were locked in from 1 AM until 5 AM, the waterings had started exactly 12 days ago and it was not only this strange rain and these "Waterers" walking around our crops and around our homes, but it was also a time of pure collective psychosis, things were happening that we had never seen before, suicides and criminality had increased even in the most peaceful regions and the rate had risen to levels never seen before.

Every day it was more difficult to distinguish between what was real and what was part of what the news reported, "hallucinations product of unfounded terror", but I refused to believe that everything that had been happening for 12 days was part of my mind, I was seeing it with my own eyes and feeling it with my body, something was clearly not right here, healthy people were suddenly starting to die, this "acid rain" was coming from these lights that were going back and forth, they were swinging in the dark sky, but they were also swinging along large surfaces close to the ground.

The one in the skies looked like "stars" that seemed to act in a planned way, but why weren't we doing anything about it? The news from the beginning and throughout the day spoke of emergency meetings by the important leaders of the great "Center-Regions" but nothing was being done. Our armed forces also did not seem to know or did not want to fight these lights with the false idea that it was a natural process, which mysteriously happened in every corner of the "Known Lands" exactly at 03:00 AM and ended at the same time.

The "spectacles" of these strange lights seemed to intensify every day, or at least that's what I believed together with some of my neighbors, but most of the people, although they were uneasy, did not seem to rebel against this phenomenon, some out of fear and others out of subordination. Also, as I was saying before, helped by the news by misinforming through supposedly renowned "scientists" who loudly commented publicly that this irrigation had already happened several times many years ago and that it was something normal, but the reality is that none of it was.

The clock struck 02:59AM, and while I was begging in my interior for prayers one after the other, I was screaming in my mind that please this time those lights would not appear, that the damned "Red Watering" would end once and for all. I felt in this deep terror that something was really being hidden and that they were killing us in silence, that it was all part of a macabre plan to assassinate us all in conjunction with the leaders of these "Center-Regions".

My father slept, I don't really know how he managed to fall asleep, I think that the media sooner or later end up making you docile and servile after so many years listening to them. I also think that maybe he preferred to immerse himself and believe in these big media that acted and were ready to put in your mind whatever came from the top, and today was no exception since they somehow brought the necessary tranquility both to his interior and to almost all the population in general, They kept us or tried to keep us in this state, repeating over and over again that these rains were natural due to a phenomenon they called "EDA" and that it could happen every so often, but how could something natural happen for so many days in a row, always at exactly the same time? Something clearly didn't add up, healthy people were suddenly getting sick all around.

At first we didn't believe this version so much, but after 6-7 days we all knew someone who was getting seriously ill. There were neighbors who were dying since those strange rains started watering us, and they always lasted exactly twenty minutes, all watering ended at 03:20 and those thick grey clouds also dissipated in the distance. My tremors came back, always since that fateful December 25th where it all started, it was 03:00 AM and at that moment nothing else mattered but to put my forehead against the small window on my right, and just watch, and pray... pray that this time nothing would happen.

My mind remembered again and again that "Pillar of Fire" that had taken place in another important Center-Region four days ago, or those strange gases that seemed to come out of the earth itself in distant earthquakes in the South, why did these events happen? And why did it seem that the great leaders who made decisions acted as if everything was natural? Many of these questions were going to take some time to arrive, but they would arrive.

CHAPTER 36 - FIRE ON THE WALLS AND POISONOUS IRRIGATION

The rain began to fall, drop after drop that accumulated along with my disappointment, again to go through this? I asked myself internally, I was really exhausted and with a lot of dread, it was not for less, a night that I would never forget was coming and everything would begin at this precise moment.

The drops of this supposed "poisonous irrigation" were falling again, but this time they were going to be accompanied. The immense columns that divided our regions and the walls that limited them began to catch fire completely and this irrigation instead of extinguishing it made the flames ignite with more and more intensity and expanded rapidly.

The dark night that was only illuminated by the holographic lunar sphere there in the heavens contemplated that furious fire that first illuminated the horizon and then seemed to slowly extinguish, all this was the harbinger of an announced end and that few had known how to interpret. I tried so many times to leave my home, from my window I saw the intense fire and then the sudden watering that fell with more intensity in some spotlights, but among the smoke I observed the shadows of the vile waterers that walked through the fields from one side to the other, they made noise like the legs of insects under the wood. I cringed so many times that I also hurt my hands pressing against that window without even noticing it.

I could not leave my father, who was sleeping in the next room without even knowing what was happening, I knew immediately, I feared it since the beginning of this hell, nothing of what was happening was natural and those sprinklers were present in great numbers in front of everyone's sight. In some strange way I felt inside me a great relief, everyone now knew the truth, although many would never be able to tell it.

The great column still had fire that went from almost its beginning to the middle of its path, it could be seen in the distance, it gave way and fell without mercy, seeing this the alarm of danger was lit throughout the City-Region, and as if it were an intruder, other bells began to ring in the distance. The fields were infested with these "Watering" beings that walked around with strange devices that emanated gases, they were not well distinguished but the amount of that night was superior even to the total of all the previous days. That day I felt what I had feared weeks ago, they were certainly killing us all.

When I saw that the situation was critical and that the usual twenty minutes had passed and none of this stopped, I ran to my father Gerald's room, I can't even explain today why it took me so long to come out of that shock, but I was terrified, so much so that my body seemed paralyzed for those minutes. I shouted to my father to wake up and that we had to leave urgently, the front door began to be hit hard, the alarm outside and the home-scanners sounded in unison, everything began to live in slow motion, between dazed and confused I could see that the "Regadores" entered our house.

CHAPTER 37 - PATAGONIAN GIANTS DEFEND HUMAN LANDS

Two beings entered and began to spray with those toxic gases, I put a mask on my father who just woke up sleepy without understanding the situation, while trying to do the same I was able to locate mine and then close the door of the room. I signaled my father that he should be quiet, and we both melted into an absolute sepulchral silence, the kind that lasts seconds, but your whole life flashes before you.

Deafening sirens and alarms could be heard outside, as the explosions began, but what would those explosions be? we wondered. At that moment it mattered little because the main danger was just behind the door, a creature was walking down the hallway outside while with my father in silence we waited for the worst, in that moment of desperation I looked out the window and the shadows of the Regadores were now accompanied by others, some giant shadows were present. I signaled again to my father so that he could observe it, could it be that our prayers had been heard? The "Patagones" or "Archons" were fighting, defending the human lands, those beings that, always far from humanity, lived in solitude in the cold south, and today they were here with us, trying the impossible, a battle that seemed lost from the very beginning.

The two beings we had in our home shot out, an unknown sound invaded the outside, I guess it was the call of one of their leaders or something warning them about the danger. They needed all the Regadores there since an unexpected visitor had appeared, these giants had no mercy whatsoever and while many fell by the gases that emanated and the blue rays of some kind of weaponry that these beings brought, many others were still knocking down Regadores with their overwhelming force, the difference in physical strength was abysmal in comparison.

I opened the door in panic and amazement but with some hope, I did not see any being crossing the door, I signaled again to my father and we tried to go out, although at that time we did not really know if we were better off outside or inside our home, but after that experience of confinement waiting for death before those creatures, we decided to go out and join somehow to those Giant Archons that gathered groups of humans around to help them.

CHAPTER 38 - ESCAPING WITH THE ARCHONS

We ran outside with all our energy towards a column with a tiled roof, there was no longer that rain, but we left our masks on because that deadly gas still existed in the atmosphere, and we did not even know the real symptoms that caused it. My father was already a bit older, he had turned 156 that year and although he was still physically well with the mask on, his vision was limited and he fell into the mud and the intense rain that had fallen minutes before.

I could see that he was trying to get up and place the mask that had almost come off his face, he was full of mud and I could not see anything at all, I tried to go back, but the figure of a giant stood next to me and extending one of his arms at a great distance, he stopped my intentions to move and kept me next to that column. Another Archon was on his way to save my father, but reddish-blue lightning bolts began to rain from a far distance over the dark sky, those penetrating the ground like raindrops.

One of them had penetrated the giant who was falling with signs of pain, and another had pierced the chest of my father who was lying on the cold ground. Regardless of the pressure the giant exerted on me, I made movements to escape from him and ran towards my father, taking off his mask I could see his face, and I understood that he was no longer among us, I took his hand and embraced his body knowing that I would never see him again. I could not understand the evil that was falling on me, this terror that stood in the way of human destiny that night and that we were all living, I removed my mask to embrace the body of my dead father, Gerald I shouted loudly looking at the dark sky without moon, why are we living this misfortune? Why the human has to live this end?

One of the Giants was lying next to my father, and his face was near my left foot, among all my confusion and absolute sadness I could see his face up close, he had stone features like a "Golem" from the stories my father told me, that with his outstretched arms he simulated that flight of his soul, that he was returning to the source of the Heavenly Lands and that sometime I will also return to meet him.

But not that night, it was not the time for me, because that Archon who also saved my life, took me with force of my torn clothes and took me to the group of several people that were formed simulating a large circle. Surrounded by a great wall of Giants that continued fighting against those tireless Regadores that returned again and again to try to penetrate to annihilate the few surviving humans that we were there.

Once inside the circle, many other neighbors that I knew along with other people from other Regions began to join our group, all of us with tears of pain on our muddy faces, without masks or any protection, we moved in unison with those Giants that acted as a wall and prevented any enemy attack. Reddish rays were falling from the skies and I cannot be sure even today about the Archon technology, but a great protective shield seemed to impede the passage and extinguished the forces of those deadly rays over our heads.

There were many children running with us in awe, I held the hand of one of them to make him feel some calm, all that was the strangest and most horrible thing that our humanity has ever gone through. The rescue of those giants in all the Regions was a heroic act of which I believe we will never be able to repay, a genuine and unconditional act of love for humanity, because it should be clarified that all the Archons/Patagons we knew lived far away in the south and could have escaped without us, we were only a few thousand, but we were able to start again, they gave us the possibility of a new beginning.

CHAPTER 39 - THE IMMENSE TREE MADE OF LIGHTS - THE BRIDGE TO ASGARD

After a while of hurrying we began to walk more slowly, many of us had taken the younger children in our arms since that walk seemed to have no end, I am not sure how long we had been on that road, but with the fear that instilled all the situation we were living around us I really lost count. I would only know that we had crossed large plots of land by looking at my injured feet, which were bleeding from the wounds along with the soaked mud.

The Giants were still walking alongside us, and were all around us in every direction as they covered our passage. We had stopped receiving those rays from the heavens, the rain had stopped and there was no strange gas in the atmosphere but there was fog that night and at dawn it began to become more and more noticeable. The Archons that were to our North put their arms up in the air as a sign that we should stop completely, so we did while they made their way generating a path for us to enter. A metallic fortification was born before our eyes, its doors wide open awaited our entrance. We did not know where we were going but no one wanted to be left out and alone in those lands that had become inhospitable to all mankind.

While I was entering I could observe everything around, on the outside that fortification that seemed to be made of crystalline limestone was shining, but inside the walls changed to a darker tone, with points of blue light at all angles that filled the upper part, like a holographic sky full of bright stars, for a moment I felt I was entering a small "land" within our own land.

When all the humans and Giants entered there, some of those bright blue lights of this artificial sky gathered in the center forming an immense tree, its roots penetrating the ground and forming its extension to heights that were even difficult to observe. A blue and immense glowing tree was born before our eyes that could not believe their eyes. A robotic and deep voice interrupted our contemplation, indicating that we had to enter there, some doors opened from the base of that tree made of lights, and we were all incredibly confused.

A war of human annihilation was going on outside, millions had died and among them my dear father, and now a group of thousands of survivors were in a fortification of the Archons in front of a tree created by artificial lights. My confused mind could not understand it. We all looked at each other without understanding anything at all, the children covered their muddy faces because of fear, the Giants indicated us with their hands that we should enter there, I remembered then the stories that my father told me as a child and that I believe we had all heard at some time during our lives. Were we perhaps entering the Great World Tree and Bridge to the first lands of Asgard? Were these giant fortifications part of the Hyperborean Lands?

The first humans who entered there somehow "became" also thousands of points of light, somehow mimicked with that great tree and artificial stars. They were disappearing one by one, there was certainly an atrocious fear inside me, but also the hope of a new life, incredibly for my confused mind that knew that outside the human world was being destroyed in a thousand pieces and that the past of just a few hours no longer existed. It was my turn to enter, together with the boy I had helped to get there who was holding my hand tightly.

My whole body was completely illuminated, I could see while this was happening and I was now converted into thousands of points of light, my hand was melting with the hand of the child who was also, an abysmal darkness around us succumbed, I no longer felt fear, nor pain, nor cold nor hunger, nor the hardships and sadness of what had happened, two large doors opened and a bright sun came in almost blinding my sight, Then I could observe everything, it was exactly as my father had told me, I could deduce it then, we were at the gates of Asgard and as we walked along those roads made of stone, many other humans welcomed us with a smile and patted us on the back, somehow they knew of our pain, I understood then that another life was about to begin.

CHAPTER 40 - MESSAGE FROM HELEN MORRIS

The new humanity seems to have forgotten the true path and the path that their ancestors have left to walk it, rather it was not forgotten, but buried by the same conquering parasites, as in these writings and in many other ancestral writings we observe that the old humanity always fought against this reigning power, in our days outside the Ice Walls our humanity helps each other, moves away from objects, from the material, is interested in the welfare of the other, does not compete, has no desire for power and the fictitious growth that is supposed to grant that paper money they use, has no greed, It does not interpose or use any type of leadership to step on the dreams and destiny of any other being, that is far from the reality of the new humanity in its walled lands, and we must begin to realize that a life like ours is possible, we are human and brothers, and although our growth both in there by our ancestors and out here now by us has been different, the true human essence is the one that pursues the dream of freedom and that comes closer every day, although the environment seems so dark and desolate, we know that we can all together change this reality and return to understand the essence of the true being, the one that comes from and will always be connected to the Celestial Lands.

ABOUT THE AUTHOR

Claudio Nocelli

Born in Buenos Aires, Argentina,

Lover of occult stories since I was a child, I followed the skies closely after spending hours reading about UFOs and everything related to extraterrestrials. But something did not fit me in those interspatial travels until the story of the navigator would finally dispel so many doubts, in addition to the ideas of ancient books of mythology and travel that created a possible connection with lands and planets behind the Poles, everything began to have another perspective and sense, especially regarding the human past and the infinite spiritual potential.

As we all know the channels that talk about certain topics and do it with great respect, may not be so well received by the mainstream media, for this reason if any link of our social networks is not working we will always try to have the website active.

Creator of the YouTube Channel: "Nos Confunden" and "Nos Confundieron" with more than 6,300,000 views and the website: nosconfunden.com.ar that we invite everyone to join to continue growing.

BOOKS BY THIS AUTHOR

The Navigator Who Crossed The Ice Walls: Worlds Beyond The Antarctica

The story of navigator William Morris who, after the Independence War in the United States, decides to investigate with his new vessel the waters surrounding the Antarctic Circle, finding an unknown passage to an open sea. Other lands await him behind, along with another civilization, the story will begin to reveal to the entire group another reality based on the true past and future of the human being. It will finally lead him to the discovery of other worlds behind the Antarctica and most importantly to know himself, a unique journey from which nothing will ever be the same again.

BOOKS BY THIS AUTHOR

Terra-Infinita, Extraterrestrial Worlds And Their Civilizations: The Story Told By The Woman Who Was Born In The Lands Behind The Ice Walls

The story told by the woman who comes from the lands behind the ice walls, in the "Ancestral Republic", daughter of the navigator William Morris, who will provide information that was hidden from us for a long time about the worlds that are crossing the poles and the secrets of extraterrestrial civilizations. We will also be able to discover the human history before the Last Reset and the continuation of what happened to her father when he returned to our lands. This can change everything.

BOOKS BY THIS AUTHOR

The Lands Of Mars: 178 Worlds Under The Great Dome

178 Worlds Under the Great Dome - Volume 1 - The Collection of the hidden Books about lands beyond the ICE WALLS
The lands of Mars hide much more than we imagine, here we can read the stories of the origin of the Martians in conjunction with the ancestral expeditions of the humans who live behind the Ice Walls.

Chapt. 1 - Where does the information from the Other Worlds come from?
Chapt. 2 - MARS, A Great Zoo
Chapt. 3 - The "Red Planet" Stained with Innocent Blood
Chapt. 4 - The Ancestral Expedition, The Writings of Captain Roald
Chapt. 5 - The Ship of Repentance Ones
Chapt. 6 - The Portal Hidden on Mars
Chapt. 7 - The Dark Membrane - Information Behind The Great Dome

Printed in Great Britain
by Amazon

26755350R00116